"It looks **everything just right."**

"You bet you did," Drew answered bitterly as Traig came out of the kitchen.

His welcoming expression vanished. "Would it help if I said I don't know what the hell you're talking about?"

"You came here to find evidence to discredit me," Drew reminded him.

"Not to discredit you — to establish the truth. I still intend to do that."

"I see," she said dully.

"You see what?"

"Where I stand with you. You'll stop at nothing to establish the truth, even if it means hurting me. So how can I be sure you wouldn't also sell me poor-quality steel to harm my project?"

"Because I damned well told you I didn't!" he exploded. "It's up to you to decide whom you're going to trust."

Man and Wife

Valerie Parv

Harlequin Books

TORONTO • NEW YORK • LONDON
AMSTERDAM • PARIS • SYDNEY • HAMBURG
STOCKHOLM • ATHENS • TOKYO • MILAN

Original hardcover edition published in 1984
by Mills & Boon Limited

ISBN 0-373-02693-5

Harlequin Romance first edition May 1985

CHAPTER ONE

'GOOD morning, Miss Dominick. Congratulations—the news is in all the papers.'

'Thanks, Geoff.' Drew smiled warmly at the elderly security man as she stepped out of the carpark lift. Several brisk strides brought her to another bank of elevators. As she waited for a lift to arrive, she looked around idly.

The lobby was filling with employees arriving for work and she returned their friendly but deferential greetings, noting without concern the wary appraisal of the more junior among them. She was accustomed to the mixed reaction. The headquarters of Dominick Developments had been her second home long before her father died so she had grown up among these people, knowing that she would one day run the corporation alone.

Her corporation. She felt the warm glow of possession as she surveyed the lobby, gateway to the Dominick property development empire.

It was certainly an impressive gateway. The glass walls of the circular lobby looked out over Sydney's traffic-clogged Bond Street, and framed the bulk of the Stock Exchange Centre. In the centre of the lobby a splash of morning sunshine fell like a spotlight on to the entwined pair of capital Ds woven into the carpet. They were the company's symbol and, not entirely coincidentally, her own initials.

The elevator doors slid open and the other intending passengers stood back to let her go in first.

With the ease of long habit she did so and nodded at the lift driver. 'Tower please, Don.'

She was the last to leave the lift, the employees all getting off at lower floors. The topmost floor was her domain, known by one and all as the Ivory Tower, partly because of its location which commanded the finest view in the building but also because of its ivory decor, Drew's favourite colour.

Her assistant, Maggie Symmonds, peered at her over rimless glasses as she entered the outer office. 'Congratulations, Drew. You must be on top of the world this morning.'

Drew passed a hand over her eyes. 'I'm a bit too tired for that. Coming on top of all the work we've had to put in to win the award, last night's presentation was the limit.'

Maggie clucked her tongue sympathetically then frowned. 'In that case, perhaps you'd better not look at the papers this morning. They're all on your desk, but. . . .'

'Inky Hedges again? I saw him scribbling frantically all through the dinner.'

Maggie nodded. 'I'm afraid so. What did you ever do to that man to make him so antagonistic towards you?'

'I don't know, Maggie, really,' Drew sighed. In truth, she did know but she wasn't going to give Hedges the satisfaction of the publicity. He was the one who made the pass at her at an industry dinner months ago, and he shouldn't have been surprised when she turned him down flat. But his ego had been wounded as she learned to her cost when the sniping editorials about her began to appear in his weekly gossip column. She moved reluctantly towards her own office. 'I'd better see what he's raked up this time.'

Watching her go, Maggie allowed her deep concern for Drew to show on her face now the object of it could no longer see it. Ever since she was a child, Drew had hated anyone to fuss over her so Maggie had developed the habit of shielding her thoughts. She had watched Drew grow from awkward, coltish adolescence to capable, confident womanhood, yet Drew never allowed the world to see what a struggle she had found it, with only her forceful father for guidance. Maggie often wondered what Drew would have been like if her mother had lived. She would almost certainly have benefited from a greater female influence. Oh, she knew how to shoot, fish, ride and run a corporation as well as any man. But when it came to handling emotional crises. . . .

'I can almost hear what you're thinking, Maggie,' came Drew's voice from the connecting doorway. 'I'm perfectly all right, I assure you. Just tired, that's all.'

'If you could hear my thoughts this minute, you'd be blushing scarlet, young woman,' Maggie responded tartly.

Grinning cheekily at her, Drew waltzed into her own office and closed the door. Maggie had been her father's secretary for more years than she could remember, and had been the nearest thing to a confidante Drew had ever had. It was only natural that the other woman should continue to work for Drew after her father died nearly two years ago. She was one of a handful of employees who called Drew by her given name and was the only one who could get away with handing out advice, whether it was wanted or not. Drew couldn't imagine what she would have done without dear Maggie.

Drew's office, like its owner, was neat and businesslike. A wall of windows looked out across the city to the Harbour, providing a stunning backdrop for the furniture she had chosen herself. Half of the room was furnished with an Italian crystal table she used for meetings. It was complemented on the other side by a handsome two-toned desk and rust-coloured velvet chairs.

On the desk were piled the newspapers Maggie had suggested she ignore. For the merest moment, she was tempted. Inky Hedges had a vicious pen which could pierce like an arrow. Then Andrew Dominick's voice came back to her, 'A Dominick never turns his back on a fight.'

Or in this case, *her* back, she thought with a grimace. Resignedly she sat down at her desk and unfolded the *Sydney Tribune*. The article under Inky's byline leapt out at her from the inside front page. 'Double D wins WBG Award', the headline said cryptically. Translated, it meant her company had won the coveted Walter Burley Griffin award and, with it, a contract to build the largest trade complex in the southern hemisphere.

'What scandal have you come up with this time?' she said aloud to the page as she settled down to read. The strain created by the last few months of working for the award made the print swim before her eyes and she had to blink hard to bring it into focus.

Ten minutes later she jumped to her feet, crumbling the article into a ball and hurling it across the desktop. 'Damn it! It's not fair!' she cried.

At once the door opened and Maggie came in. 'I take it you've read Mr Hedges' purple prose?' she said calmly.

'Prose? That isn't prose. It's ... it's character assassination!' she seethed. 'That narrow-minded, chauvinistic. . . .'

'He's all that and then some,' Maggie agreed.

Drew looked at her assistant in astonishment. 'How

can you take this so calmly? Look!' With shaking hands she smoothed out the crumpled sheet and spread it in front of Maggie. 'He wrote not a word about our design for the Centre which the judges said was one of the most innovative concepts they'd ever seen. Nothing about the months of work, the planning, the feasibility studies—or even the competition we had to beat to pull it off.'

Distractedly, she ran a hand through her glossy black hair, jumbling it into urchin spikes. 'All he talks about is what I wore, my hairdo my make-up—or lack of it, in his estimation. Read this part.'

She stabbed a finger at one paragraph and Maggie leaned across the desk to read the offending copy.

'Miss Dominick—if, it was Miss and not Mister (the hair is so short it is difficult to tell)—accepted the award with the grace of an ugly duckling. On an occasion which would have merited at least a new gown, for any other woman, she saw fit to wear an outfit which was more familiar to those present than the lady's own features. One can't help wondering if a swan will ever emerge from under the steel exterior of our best-known lady tycoon.'

'I've a good mind to sue him.'

'We've been through this before,' Maggie reminded her gently. She, too, was shocked by the columnist's vitriole. 'But it's a syndicated column and he can write pretty much what he likes as long as it is identified as opinion and not fact.'

'Surely he didn't have to be so cruel! I know I'm no oil painting, but. . . .'

'Now that's enough of that,' Maggie intervened. 'You're a perfectly lovely young woman. And you turn yourself out very well, especially when you consider that most women your age have nothing else to worry about except their own looks. Just remember, you could take the place of any of those beauties Hedges uses in his centrefolds, but I wonder how many of them could run a corporation like this one?'

Drew gave her a look of pure gratitude. 'Thanks, Maggie,' she said fervently. 'I don't know if any of that's true but it's good for my ego to hear you say it.'

'Just take a good look in your bathroom mirror and you'll see if it's true or not.'

Drew didn't need to go near a mirror to know what it would tell her. She had studied her own features often enough to know exactly what she would see there. Framed in the glass would be a tall woman, almost six feet in her stockinged feet, painfully slender with an oval face whose natural hollows at the temples, cheekbones and jawline gave her the look of a piece of sculpture, the main redeeming feature being huge green eyes fringed by spectacularly long lashes. With no mother or sisters to guide her, she had no idea whether this combination added up to beauty or not. 'He's right about one thing,' she said ruefully, 'I wasn't looking my best last night and they *had* all seen that dress before.'

'It wasn't your fault that Millie chose last night to quit on you with no warning,' Maggie defended her staunchly.

'Oh, I've had warning enough. She hates dogs and ever since I got Bosun, she's been threatening to quit. I think when he ate the roast she was defrosting for dinner, it was the last straw.'

'But he's just a puppy. He can't help his instincts.'

Drew looked at Maggie fondly. 'You'd defend me to the death, wouldn't you, no matter what the circumstances?'

'It's my job,' the other woman said gruffly. 'That Millie had no sense of responsibility.'

'You'd never walk out like that, I know,' Drew agreed, pressing the other woman's hand. 'But let's face it, there aren't many people in the world like you.'

'If the mutual admiration society's over, Garth Dangerfield would like a meeting with you this morning,' Maggie said, plainly embarrassed.

Equally glad of the change in subject, Drew flicked her glance to the calender on her desk. 'He'll be anxious to get the project underway now we've actually got the contract. You can tell him I'll see him at ten.'

At the door, Maggie turned. 'You know what you need?' she mused.

'No, what?'

'A wife.'

Drew grinned. 'A husband, you mean? Oh, Maggie, not you, too!'

'No, I meant a wife. Not in the literal sense, of course. But think about it. A husband would have his own career and interests. What you need is a wife, someone who'll put *your* interests first. A man in your position would never have to worry about domestic details, or what to do if the hired help quit without notice. He'd have a woman at home taking care of all that, not to mention massaging his ego at the same time.'

'I didn't know you were such a feminist,' laughed Drew.

'I'm not—just fair-minded.'

When Maggie had gone, Drew went into her private bathroom and plugged in her electric kettle. Someone from the executive dining room would have brought her coffee if she'd rung for it, but she preferred to do this chore herself. It gave her time to think without interruption.

While she waited for the water to boil, she thought

about Maggie's suggestion. It was impossible, of course, but it would be bliss to have someone at home to handle all the domestic details Drew found so irritatingly time consuming. When Andrew Dominick was alive, she couldn't remember him ironing his own clothes or cooking a meal for guests. Millie had fussed over him like a mother hen. It was only when Drew succeeded him as her employer that Millie started to be difficult, setting out what she would or wouldn't do so Drew ended up doing half the work herself to avoid arguments.

Imagine having a man at home who was as selflessly devoted to Drew as Millie had been to her father! He would make no demands on her, expect no more from her than she was prepared to give. She would come home to a gourmet meal cooked and waiting, a drink poured and ready to hand—and there would be no repetition of last night's fiasco.

The memory made her shudder with distaste. She had come home exhausted. A sudden upward movement in world steel prices had threatened months of work on Pacific Centre, the company's entry in the Walter Burley Griffin Award. She and Garth Dangerfield had spent half the day on the telephone ensuring that their suppliers would honour their quoted prices if Dominick Developments won the award.

Having achieved that, she was almost too tired to go to the presentation itself. If there had been anyone who could have gone in her place, she would have given them her blessing. But even Garth Dangerfield, the young consultant who had helped develop the Dominick entry, was not well enough known in the industry to represent the company. It was her duty to go and that was that.

However, she had reckoned without the antics of

Bosun, her recently acquired pedigree long-haired dachshund. He had been wished on her by a so-called friend and Drew had been so beguiled by the puppy's liquid eyes and velvety flop-ears that she had given him a home against her better judgment. Now she was devoted to the scrap of mischief and the feeling was quite obviously mutual. Unfortunately, the housekeeper didn't share her enthusiasm.

Millie met her at the front door, wearing her hat and coat and with a suitcase on the floor beside her. As soon as she caught sight of Drew she launched into a tirade about the dog's misdeeds then announced that she wasn't putting up with it any longer. 'I gave you fair warning, Miss Dominick. You had the choice of that dog or me.'

'You can't be leaving, Millie. However will I replace you at such short notice?'

'With respect, Miss, that's your problem. Of course, you could get rid of the dog then I might consider staying on.'

Drew knew Millie would never have dared give her father such an ultimatum. He would have sent her on her way for even thinking about it. Still, Drew hesitated. Replacing Millie was going to be enormously difficult. She found herself wavering. Then Bosun, alerted by the sound of his beloved mistress's voice, came hurtling between Millie's legs to reach Drew.

As she crouched down to gather him up, her resolve hardened. Bosun had more love and loyalty for her in one paw than Millie would ever know. 'I'm not parting with the dog,' she said, standing up.

'In that case, goodbye Miss,' Millie said with a catch in her voice. She had obviously expected Drew to cave in at the first sign of opposition. Now she stood hesitantly on the doorstep. 'About my outstanding wages. . . .'

'Come inside for a moment and I'll write you a cheque,' Drew said at once.

Moments later, clutching the cheque, Millie padded off down the driveway towards a waiting taxi.

Resisting an urge to call her back, Drew clutched Bosun's warm body tightly. 'It's just you and me now, boy,' she said into his silky coat.

For answer Bosun licked her face with his rough tongue, making her laugh until she put him down in self-defence. As she blotted her face with a handkerchief she caught sight of the grandfather clock in the hall. 'Good grief! There's less than an hour before I'm due at the Hilton,' she told the little dog in dismay.

The extent of Millie's defection only became apparent when Drew hurried upstairs to her bedroom. The gown she had planned to wear tonight still lay in its nest of tissue in the box. She had expected to find it pressed and waiting for her to slip into.

Snatching it up, she flew back down the stairs to the utility room with Bosun panting at her heels.

Millie made ironing look so easy, she recalled as she got out the equipment and plugged in the iron. She had done the chore so few times herself that for a moment, she couldn't remember where she was supposed to add the water for steam. After a couple of clumsy attempts, she got the iron filled and all the knobs set at the right places, but just as she began her task the telephone rang.

'Damn!' she said, startling Bosun who looked at her anxiously. She reached down and fondled him. 'This is all your fault you know.'

He didn't look in the least penitent but led the way to the shrilling telephone and barked at it until Drew picked up the receiver. It was Garth Dangerfield.

'I just wanted to wish you well for tonight,' he assured her.

'You're still coming, aren't you?' she asked, surprised.

'Of course. But I won't be at the head table like you bigwigs, so I thought I'd give you my good wishes now, in case we don't get a chance to talk later.'

'That was very sweet of you, Garth. Thanks,' she said, warmed by his gesture. As she replaced the receiver, a horrid chemical smell reached her nostrils. 'Oh lord, my dress!'

She rushed back to the ironing board but the cloud of smoke and the burning smell told her there was no need to hurry. The iron lay face-down on the gown which was ruined beyond repair. 'Of all the times for this to happen!' she wailed at Bosun. He wagged his tail uncertainly. 'It's all very well for you. You don't have to worry about five-hundred-dollar gowns, do you? One fur coat lasts you a lifetime.'

Miserably, she switched off the iron and dropped the smouldering remains of the dress into the dustbin. So much for making a splash at the awards dinner tonight!

By the time she had changed into another gown—a strapless black sheath she had worn on several other occasions, but which was thankfully crushproof, she was running hopelessly late. She had barely enough time to comb her hair into some semblance of order and dash on some make-up, before the car arrived to take her to the dinner.

Even if he had known the whole story, Inky Hedges wouldn't have taken it into consideration before he slandered her appearance, she thought despondently. The kettle's piercing whistle brought her back to the present. As Maggie pointed out, men like him made sure they had dependable domestic back-up so they were never faced with the kind of crisis she'd had last night.

No, they weren't, were they? So why should she put up with it? Her father had brought her up believing that anything you didn't like, you should at least try to change. But did she have the courage to flout convention and hire herself a man? In her present mood, she had the courage to try anything.

'Maggie, you're a genius!' she said aloud. Before she had time for second thoughts, she switched off the kettle and hurried back to her desk where she picked up the phone. 'Get me the Bell Recruitment Service, please,' she instructed Maggie.

Moments later, Colleen Bell's voice came on the line. 'Good morning, Miss Dominick. I suppose you're calling about the short list of applicants for the valuer's position?'

'No, our personnel department's taking care of that,' Drew assured her. 'I have a personal request, something I'd like you to handle for me yourself.'

'Sounds intriguing,' Colleen said warily. 'What is the position you want filled?'

Drew took a deep breath. 'I've decided I need a wife,' she said with forced lightness.

There was a long silence. 'You did say wife?'

Quoted back at her by someone else, it did sound like an absurd request. Then her gaze rested on Hedges' insulting article and her resolve hardened. 'That's right. It's not as wild as it sounds. What I want is someone to take over the running of my life away from the office.'

'Oh, you mean a housekeeper,' Colleen said, sounding relieved.

'Actually, I need something more than that. This time, I want someone who's prepared to put my needs ahead of his own.'

Colleen cleared her throat. 'Wait a minute. You said *his*?'

'Mmm-hmm. I want a man who can do for me everything that a wife does for a man if he had a job like mine. Things like entertaining, domestic chores, personal shopping, moral support—you name it.'

'I see,' Colleen said slowly, although it was plain from her tone that she didn't really. 'It might prove to be a tall order. We don't get many men with a range of skills like that on our books, even in these liberated times.'

'Are you telling me you can't do it?' Drew asked silkily.

'Oh, no,' Colleen said at once. Dominick Developments was one of her biggest clients so she wouldn't want to risk losing them to another agency by admitting any request was beyond her. 'It just might . . . er . . . take a little time, that's all,' she tailed off.

'Take all the time you need.' She was about to hang up when Colleen's voice halted her.

'Oh, er . . . one other thing.'

'Yes Colleen?'

'This . . . arrangement you have in mind, it . . . er . . . doesn't include any . . . that is, I mean. . . .'

'If you mean does it include sex—no,' Drew said as she realised what the other woman was driving at. 'The term "wife" was meant purely to give you an idea of the breadth of his duties, so you wouldn't think I wanted ordinary domestic help. I don't plan to marry the man in the literal sense.'

'Good, I'm glad we're clear about that.'

Drew smiled wryly as she hung up the phone. She could almost hear Colleen thinking—poor Drew, so desperate for a man in her life that she has to hire one. The agent probably thought she wanted a gigolo, and was too afraid of losing a valuable client to voice her misgivings. Drew looked distastefully at the Hedges' article. What would he make of her request if he knew about it?

Only then did the full extent of what she had done come home to her and she stared at the phone in horror. She had just rung the company's recruiting consultants and asked them to hire a man to run her private life! How on earth could she have let herself get so angry over a newspaper article as to not only consider hiring a male wife, but to set the wheels in motion? What if they actually found somebody?

Then common sense came to her aid. Where would they find a man willing to put his own interests second to hers? Even if he possessed the required domestic skills, no man would demean himself to that extent. Any man who would, she was bound to despise on sight.

She was worrying needlessly. In a week's time, Colleen would call her back and admit defeat and the whole silly impulse would be forgotten. If she hadn't been so overworked lately she wouldn't even have made the call in the first place.

Her intercom buzzed and she flipped the switch. 'Yes, Maggie?'

'Garth Dangerfield is here for your meeting.'

'Good. Ask him to come in.'

After only six months with Dominick Developments, Garth had proved so valuable that he was now answerable only to Drew herself. Much of the innovative thinking behind Pacific Centre had been Garth's.

Drew found his originality refreshing and had enjoyed working with him on the project. Now he was to be its co-ordinator, responsible for turning Pacific Centre from an idea on paper into a multi-million dollar reality.

She knew Garth was attracted to her. Several times

as they worked on the project, he had let her know he wanted to put their relationship on to a more personal footing but, so far, she had resisted the change. She wasn't even quite sure why. He was good looking enough, although shy and boyish at times. And they had a common bond in their work.

The few times when she had gone out with him after work she had enjoyed his company. Still, there was something indefinable in his character which made her wary of becoming too deeply involved with him. Nevertheless she looked up and smiled as he came in. 'Good morning, Garth.'

'Good morning, Drew.' He noted the crumpled paper spread out on her desk. 'Don't take any notice of that weasel. You were splendid last night.'

'Largely thanks to you,' she conceded. 'Let's face it, if it hadn't been for your ideas, we'd never have won the award.'

He avoided meeting her eyes, embarrassed by her praise, she assumed. 'Well you were the one who first thought of combining a residential component with the trade centre. The judge representing the City Council made a big thing of that aspect, how it would help revitalise the inner city and so on.'

'There were so many people in on the project, I can't take the credit,' he demurred.

'But you can't stop me giving it to you,' she insisted, smiling at him. He would have to learn not to be so modest if he was to go very far in this business.

They moved to the crystal table and sat down. Garth opened a folder and spread the contents out in front of them. 'This is our formal acceptance for the award,' he explained. 'Once we sign it, we're bound by its conditions until the project is completed.'

She reached for a pen. 'Then let's get on with it.'

'Before you sign, I think you should know there's a

clause in the agreement which I object to most strongly.'

'Oh? What might that be?'

'The terms under which the final payment will be made.'

'I assume it's the usual penalty clause for running over time,' she said. 'All we have to do is make sure we complete the project on budget and on deadline, surely?'

'It's not as simple as that,' he said heavily, 'to make sure the winning company didn't underestimate either costs or construction time to give themselves an edge, the award committee has included a condition that should the project run more than ten per cent over budget or over time, we have to call in the runners-up as consultants, at our expense.'

She frowned. 'That seems harsh. Do we have to accept it?'

'If we accept the award, we have to accept all the conditions that go with it.'

'I see. Since we might end up having to work with them, who were the runners-up?'

Garth's fingers tightened on the table edge. 'Monroe Investments.'

Drew felt the colour drain from her face. 'Oh, no,' she breathed. 'Dad wouldn't have wanted me to even consider working with them.'

'Of course, it might never happen,' Garth said tentatively.

'We can't let it happen,' she said in an agonised whisper. 'Oh, Garth, what are our chances of keeping them out of it?'

'In this industrial climate, who knows?' he said unhappily. 'If we could count on no strikes or material hold-ups, I'd say no problem. We left ourselves enough room in all the estimates for price and currency fluctuations, weather delays and so on. But anything outside that could beat us. Ten per cent isn't much of a margin.'

It wasn't any sort of margin, she thought despairingly. 'Why wasn't this clause discussed before?' she asked.

'It's been there all the time. It's just so unexpected that nobody thought to look.'

'If only it was anybody other than Monroe. . . .'

Garth gave her a look of understanding. 'You can't feel any worse about it than I do, Drew. After all, young Monroe was the bastard who got me fired from their organisation just because I was a favourite with the old man. Young Monroe was afraid I would jeopardise his comfortable inheritance so he trumped up a reason to get me fired.'

'I'd forgotten you have as much reason to hate them as my family does,' she said gently. 'Old Man Monroe cheated my father of most of his fortune by inveigling him into a deal that supposedly couldn't fail. At the last minute, Monroe found out something was wrong and backed out, but Dad lost nearly everything he had. It took him years to get back where he was. The Dominicks have been at daggers drawn with the Monroes ever since.' She rose, determination written in every line of her attractive features. 'We'll just have to make damned sure they have no reason to invoke the consultants clause.'

'Count on me, Drew,' Garth said firmly and gazed adoringly into her eyes in a way that reminded her of Bosun. Except that in Garth's case, she could read much more than puppy love in the look. Was she ready for a relationship with him? She wished she could make up her mind because the invitation in his eyes was so clear that it was plain he had already made up his.

The next week flew past as she and Garth attended to the myriad details needed to get Pacific Centre underway. It was such a large undertaking that the initial activity attracted the watchful eye of the news media. The State Premier turned the first sod and the Governor obtained a special temporary union membership to enable him to drive the first bulldozer on to the site.

Behind the scenes, there were detailed instructions to be provided for the co-ordination and control of the activities of the architect, consulting engineers, quality surveyor and, through the architect, the contractors.

So it came as a surprise to Drew to be told that Colleen Bell was on the phone and wanted to speak to her personally. 'Hello, Colleen, what can I do for you?' she asked, on the point of rushing to the boardroom where she was to take a meeting.

'Don't tell me you've forgotten about the special assignment you gave me?' Colleen reminded her.

'Special assignment? I don't ... oh!' Belatedly, she remembered she had asked the recruiting agency to find her a male 'wife' to take over the running of her private life. It had seemed so unlikely that they would actually find someone that she had put the whole thing out of her mind. 'Don't tell me you've found someone?'

'Yes, we have,' Colleen said happily. 'Early thirties, very presentable looking so you won't have to hide him away when you have company.'

'I wasn't looking for a centrefold,' Drew snapped back, feeling unaccountably nervous.

'His domestic skills are impeccable, too,' Colleen said, sounding slightly miffed. 'I didn't believe he could do everything he said at first, so he invited me to dinner. I've never tasted anything so marvellous in my entire life.'

'What's this paragon's name?'

Did she imagine it, or was there the slightest hesitation from Colleen's end, before the other woman said, 'Christopher Traig. He's been overseas for some time. He's most anxious to take the job.'

'Well that's something, at least.'

'You don't sound very pleased about it,' Colleen said. 'Would you prefer to interview him yourself?'

If she did that, she'd chicken out of the whole deal, she knew she would. And having asked Colleen to find someone, she would look foolish if she backed out now. It would also make life difficult for her when she needed to hire real staff in future. She forced her tone to sound calm. 'No, that won't be necessary. Your agency has never let me down before. Sign him up and send him to my home address. Do you still have the key I gave you when you staffed my last party?'

'Yes, I do, luckily. I was about to return it to you. I'll tell him to go right over and get settled in. Do you want me to sign him to the usual contract?'

There was something so absurd about the idea of signing up a male 'wife' to a contract as if he was an ordinary employee that Drew almost laughed into the phone. The wording would probably read 'till death us do part' or something like that. But she kept her thoughts to herself. 'Yes, the usual contract,' she said, and hung up.

She remained where she was, staring at the phone for some minutes before she remembered the executives waiting for her in the boardroom. She wondered what they would say if she walked in and announced that their cool, calm, self-possessed director had just hired herself a male wife.

CHAPTER TWO

FOR once Drew was thankful for the bumper-to-bumper traffic which slowed her progress along the Cahill Expressway out of the city, across the coathanger arch of the Harbour Bridge and on to the network of roads which led to her home suburb of Castlecrag. She had a lot on her mind.

For some reason, her palms felt moist and her heart thumped alarmingly until she felt like a teenager on her first date at the prospect of meeting her new employee. There was no reason for nervousness, of course. But then, he was hardly the average staff member.

What sort of man would hire himself out as a spouse to an overworked female executive—in every sense bar the physical one? He was probably a balding widower or deserted husband who wanted the security of a home without the commitment, she decided.

Come to think of it, she didn't have to go through with this if she didn't want to. All she had to do was telephone Colleen at the recruitment agency and tell her the man was unsuitable, and that she had changed her mind about looking for someone in any case.

But would that be fair to the man? He had taken the job in good faith and her father had always impressed on her the importance of fair play.

'If he was female, you wouldn't be giving it a moment's thought, would you?' she asked her image in the driving mirror. The green eyes looked back at her accusingly. 'You're prejudiced,' they flashed at her. And she was! She who had fought prejudice on her own behalf when she first stepped into her father's shoes as the head of Dominick Developments. There were many people who believed they could run the company better than an upstart female of twenty-four even though she had been in training for the job since her teens. She had needed all her own voting power and every proxy she could lay her hands on to retain control, but retain it she had. Now, eighteen months later, there wasn't a shareholder in the company who would question her right to hold her present position. She should be the last person to act out of prejudice where someone else was concerned.

With an effort, she had relaxed considerably by the time she turned into her own street and drove up the hill towards the house she had inherited from her father.

Of all the real estate that had become hers on his death this was the property she prized the most. It was one of the few remaining houses designed by her idol, the Chicago architect, Walter Burley Griffin, and dated back to the 1930s when Castelcrag had been a primitive, avant garde new suburb.

Behind a tangle of bottlebrush which marked the boundary of the property—Griffin had been totally opposed to fences—the house rose majestically, as much at home in its surroundings as the boronia, Banksia and ti-trees which grew profusely around it.

Nestling into the sloping site, the chiselled stone building reminded Drew of a Polynesian village of thatched roofs at peace with their surroundings, relaxed and content in their natural habitat.

The similarity was stringest at the roofline which was formed of six modules linked by six gently sloping roofs clad with hand-split cedar shingles. The surrounding trees were reflected in the panels of mirrored glass which followed the rooflines.

Inside, cool glass and timber formed interesting canopies overhead, opening the house to the treetops and sky, while walls of glass overhung by deep eaves overlooked the bushland greenery.

As she stepped on to the slate floor which flowed from the front door, along the gallery hall, she let out a small sigh of contentment, feeling welcomed by the house as she always did.

But this time, something was different. The tantalising smell of cooking teased at her nostrils. She sniffed appreciatively, then smiled, remembering what Colleen had said about her new employee's culinary abilities. This, she had to see for herself! She moved towards the kitchen.

If she had found Burt Reynolds working in her kitchen, she couldn't have been more taken aback. At once, her mental picture of a balding widower vanished in a puff of smoke as she contemplated the man. His back was turned to her as he bent over the island cooktop, stirring something in a saucepan. Even stooped, she could see that he was unusually tall—over six feet, most likely. A striped t-shirt stretched tautly over broad shoulders then tapered to a narrow waist and firm hips clad in the snuggest pair of blue jeans she had ever seen on a man. Involuntarily, she drew in her breath.

At the sound, he half-turned. 'Hello—Miss Dominick, I presume?'

'I ... uh ... yes. And you're?' Damn it, why was she suddenly so tongue-tied?

His momentary hesitation, quickly masked, reminded her of Colleen's reaction over the phone but it was quickly forgotten as he held out his hand. 'Christopher Traig, pleased to meet you.'

His grip was firm as he enveloped her smaller hand in the warmth of his larger one. She had to step nearer to take his hand and, up close, she discovered that, although his figure was boyish from behind, there was nothing boyish in the sculptured features which were those of a worldly wise man in his early thirties. His hair and eyebrows were chestnut brown, as was the downward-tilting moustache moulded to the curve of his upper lip. For the first time, she found herself looking slightly upwards into a man's face, for his height was more than a match for hers. The eyes which held hers in a startlingly penetrating gaze were dark, almost violet blue—the colour of the sky over the Outback at night, she thought, surprising herself.

She realised her evaluation of him had kept her hand in his for longer than politeness demanded and she drew back self-consciously. To cover her confusion she said to the room at large, 'I see you've made yourself at home, Christopher.'

'I understood that was the idea—Drew,' he said levelly. She frowned at his presumptuous use of her first name and he grinned. 'I can call you Drew, I hope—I was hired as your wife, remember? Spouses only called one another by their surnames in Victorian times.'

'The wife thing was only a figure of speech,' she protested. 'I really only wanted a . . . a housekeeper.'

'A male housekeeper who could run all the tiresome details of your private life,' he supplied. 'That's hardly the usual job specification for household help.'

'It would be if I was a man,' she retorted. Underneath his calm exterior she sensed that he was laughing at her and she felt a surge of the old defensiveness. 'Isn't that what a man expects from a wife?'

Christopher allowed himself a long and frankly appreciative appraisal of her trim figure before he answered. 'Oh, a man expects a lot more from a wife than that.'

She was annoyed to feel herself colouring hotly. This wasn't going to work out at all—she must have been mad to think it ever could. 'I told you, wife was just a figure of speech,' she said as calmly as she could. 'I should have known that a man like you would be unable to think beyond one thing.'

'Now who's making assumptions?' he demanded. 'You've just met me and already you have me pigeon-holed as a man who treats women purely as sex objects. I came here to do a job, but you're judging me on appearances. Yet you'd be the first to condemn a male executive who hired a secretary that way.'

She stared at him in astonishment, all the fight going out of her at once. 'You know, you're right,' she agreed. 'I *was* judging on appearances. Forgive me?'

'Forgiven,' he said promptly.

The smile which split his face had an energy about it which made her feel as if a sunray lamp had been turned on in the room. The glow was warm and engaging. Appearances or no, she was going to have to watch her step around Mr Christopher Traig. Within a few minutes, he had turned her anger into a plea for his forgiveness. The ready way he accepted it warned her that he was accustomed to getting his own way. That might prove to be an awkward quality in an employee.

'Now what's on your mind?' he asked.

'I was wondering why you took this job?' she blurted out. She hadn't intended to ask the question so soon, but suddenly she felt a driving need to know.

He tilted his head to one side for a moment. 'It's a challenge.'

'Working for a woman, you mean?'

'No—working for you.'

'Me? But we've only just met.'

'Ah, yes, but Drew Dominick is such a well-known figure in the business world that when this job came up I couldn't resist the chance to find out what lies behind the public face.'

A sudden suspicion made her frown. 'You're not a reporter are you?'

He spread his hands wide in a gesture which almost, but not quite convinced her he was a total innocent who was offended by her question. 'No, I'm not a reporter—cross my heart.'

She wanted to ask, 'Then what *are* you?' but before she could voice the question he swivelled back to the cooktop.

'I won't even be much of a cook if I don't give this sauce the attention it deserves,' he said over his shoulder.

'I'll leave you to it,' she said since there didn't seem to be much else she could do. But to show him that he couldn't dismiss her like this, she added, 'I'd like a pre-dinner drink on the terrace before dinner, please.'

'Dry martini?' he queried, unfazed.

She lifted an eyebrow. 'How did you know?'

'Lucky guess,' he told her and resumed his stirring.

On the way out of the kitchen she almost tripped over Bosun who was sprawled on the slate floor, sleeping off his dinner, the remains of which were evident in his bowl. Score one for Christopher, she thought wryly. Millie would never have stooped to feeding the dog. At least he and Bosun were going to get along well. Too well, since the puppy hadn't even bothered to give her his usual boisterous welcome. 'Traitor,' she whispered to him.

Upstairs, there was another surprise in store. A jade green velvet housegown lay spread out on her bed and her high-heeled slippers had been set out on the floor nearby. How on earth had Christopher known what she liked to wear around the house in the evenings? He must have gone exploring through her wardrobe. The idea brought a fresh wave of colour to her cheeks.

She tried to tell herself that it was no different from Millie laying out her father's smoking jacket and slippers but she still felt a twinge of embarrassment at the idea of Christopher rummaging through her wardrobe. A man might take such things for granted but she was going to have some trouble adjusting to the idea.

He was mixing her martini when she came into the living room beyond which was a quarry tiled terrace overlooking Sugarloaf Bay. As she came in, his eye travelled over the velvet gown, lingering on the split down one side which revealed a considerable amount of tanned thigh. But he said nothing and merely handed her the glass.

'Join me?'

He shook his head. 'I haven't quite finished preparing dinner. I didn't know what time you preferred to eat so I had everything ready early. Will eight o'clock do?'

'That will be fine,' she agreed. He wasn't to know that since her father died, about the only times she sat down to a proper dinner were when she was entertaining. Millie's cooking had been of the basic kind, extending mostly to cold roasts and salad so she wasn't used to being pampered. Something else she would have to get used to, it seemed.

'Then I'll get back to my chores. Enjoy your drink.'

The room felt acutely empty when he had gone, which was crazy—he'd only been in the house half a day. But already, she had the feeling he belonged here. With her? she asked herself, then shook herself mentally. The idea was to simplify her life by offloading some of the lesser tasks, not to complicate it even further by falling for a man who would probably be off again at the drop of a hat.

But the feeling of compatibility persisted when he came back to announce that dinner was ready. This time, she insisted that he join her. When he tried to demur, she held up a hand. 'I shan't enjoy a bite knowing that you're skulking in the kitchen by yourself,' she vowed.

He grinned. 'I've never skulked in my life.'

'Nevertheless. . . .'

'All right, I surrender. But I suspect it's really a test to see whether I can stomach my own cooking.'

Not that that proved to be much of a hardship, she found when he served their meal. Colleen was right, he was a fantastic cook. They began with an entrée of brains which were perfectly cooked and had a delicate flavour. They were topped with capers and nestled on a bed of fluffy rice.

The main course consisted of scallops of veal with crab, asparagus and the Bernaise sauce he had been preparing when she came home.

'It's gratifying to cook for someone who appreciates good food,' he commented as she sampled the dessert, a mouth-watering Zabaglione flavoured with marsala.

'What you mean is, I'm a glutton,' she laughed. The wine she had drunk with the meal was helping her to relax. She no longer felt so tense and awkward in his company.

'No, just appreciative.'

She leaned towards him, conscious of the strength of his features which were heightened by the flickering candlelight. 'Tell me, where did you learn to cook like this?'

For a moment, the shuttered expression she had glimpsed in the kitchen came back, then he relaxed with an obvious effort. 'My mother believed her son should be as self-reliant as her daughter. As long as she was alive, I had to take my turn in the kitchen and helping around the house,' he confessed.

'You were lucky, having a mother to teach you those things.'

'And you weren't?'

She shook her head. 'She died when I was born. If you know anything about the business world, you'll know my father didn't have time for anything outside it. He taught me to read a balance sheet, invest in gold futures, even shoot and fish, but he couldn't keep house or cook to save his life, so I never learned either.'

'Poor little rich girl?' he queried softly.

'No, nothing like that. I just grew up with different priorities to most females.'

'No regrets?'

She hesitated, unaware of how self-revealing the pause was. 'I don't think so,' she said finally. 'I have everything I could want.'

'Including the Walter Burley Griffin Award,' he commented idly.

She looked at him in surprise. 'You know about that?'

'I've been overseas, not on the moon. I read about it. The plan you submitted was first rate.'

The sudden edge of coolness in his voice made the compliment sound somehow insulting. 'The judges thought so,' she said stiffly then told herself she was being foolish. Maybe he had a friend at a rival company and had been hoping they would win. 'You sound like you know something about my work. Have you worked in the industry yourself?'

'I'm a qualified architect,' he admitted with seeming reluctance. 'But I haven't practised as one for a long time. I've been more on ... the administration side. I've spent most of my working life overseas.'

She felt a surge of sympathy for him. 'And when you came back you found you couldn't get a job in your own field, was that it? Maybe I can help.'

'No, I don't want you to do that,' he said quickly.

'Don't tell me you're too proud to accept help from a woman?'

'Something like that,' he said gruffly, busying himself with pouring more wine into their glasses.

Looking at his bent head, she felt an almost irresistible urge to tousle the chestnut strands between her fingers. His fierce pride struck a responsive chord in her. Despite his denial, she was sure he had been caught out by the soaring level of unemployment which had taken place since he left the country. Rather than accept unemployment benefits, he had taken the first job offering—which happened to be working for her. Maybe it was fate. He might not accept help from a woman, but she would help him somehow, although she would have to do it discreetly.

Surely one of her associates would have room for another staff member? She would ask around. Christopher need never find out that she'd had a hand in finding an opening for him. At the same time, she felt a twinge of dismay at the thought of giving him up to his own profession. She'd had only a taste of his ministrations this evening but it was enough to convince her that she would enjoy more of the same.

'What are you smiling about?' he asked, interrupting her thoughts.

'I was thinking that this must be how men like my father managed to keep their sanity—by having someone to look after them so all they had to worry about was business. I've always known that we females had a raw deal, being expected to run a business and a home with nary a slip-up, but now I can see just how cheated we've been.'

At the mention of her father, a shadow crossed Christopher's features. 'Did you know Dad?' she asked.

He nodded, his face muscles tightening. 'I knew him.' He stood up. 'I'd better clear this lot away. I turned on the spa before dinner. It should be heated by now if you'd like a dip.'

She was baffled by the swift change of subject. Her father had made many enemies during his career—what big businessman didn't?—but it sounded as if Christopher held a personal grudge against Andrew Dominick. But if so, why would he take a job working for his daughter? She followed Christopher to the kitchen and paused in the doorway. 'Have you got something against my father?' she demanded.

'Your father?' he echoed, sounding surprised at the question. 'No, of course I haven't. Why do you ask?'

She must have read something into his tone which hadn't been there at all. 'Just a silly idea I had,' she said flatly. 'Forget it.'

Still, it was hard to believe that she had misread his reaction entirely. At the first opportunity, she resolved to see Colleen at the recruitment agency and find out more about the mysterious Christopher Traig.

But there was no point in worrying about it now. As promised, the spa was bubbling merrily at a bracing temperature, she found when she dipped a toe experimentally into the water.

The spa room had its own en suite bathroom and both rooms were decorated in black, red and silver. On one side a wall of glass looked out on to a lush garden of ferns and creepers, shaded by a wall of slatted timber. Overhead, mirrored ceiling angles reflected the outdoor bushland and bubbling spa.

With a sigh of contentment, she dropped her gown on to the slate floor and stepped into the hot water, sinking slowly down until only her shoulders protruded from the water.

For at least ten minutes, she sat unmoving, while the jets of water massaged and stimulated her body. Then her reverie was interrupted by footsteps on the tiled floor.

She opened her eyes to find Christopher standing at the poolside with a brush in one hand and a bottle in the other. Without saying a word, he flicked the switch to still the turbulence, then went down on on knee behind her. She knew she should be angry at him for coming in unannounced but the words wouldn't come and she faced the fact that she welcomed his presence. Worse, her skin tingled in anticipation of his touch.

When it came, a shudder of longing passed through her and her back arched involuntarily against his hand. Whatever the lotion was, it felt icy against her hot skin. She wondered how his hands, applying the cream to her back, could be so cool when she was burning with the fire he was stoking within her.

'You're taking this wife business a bit too seriously,' she said shakily. 'What is that stuff?'

'A seaweed derivative which coaxes the body to relax,' he told her, continuing to massage the lotion into her back.

Relax? Dear God, how could she relax when she had never felt so achingly alert? It was agony to force herself to lie still while he coated her skin with the lotion, apparently with no more sense of arousal on his part than a professional masseur. Nevertheless, when he reached her breasts her pulses quickened and she covered herself defensively with her splayed fingers. 'No, don't,' she protested.

'Don't be silly, you're as tense as a cat on hot bricks,' he chided, pushing her hands aside so he could spread more of the lotion on her breasts which were swollen from the heat of the spa.

Couldn't he see that he was the cause of her tension? She had never felt so aware of anyone as she was of him, as he took the curved brush and began to work the lotion into her shoulders and breasts with firm, almost possessive strokes.

'Won't that stuff come off in the water?' she queried trying to sound calm although her breath was coming in ever-quickening gasps.

'No, it's designed to be used in water. Here, lie back will you? I can't do it properly with you hunched over like this.'

The insistent pressure of his hands on her shoulders forced her to stretch out in the water until the back of her head was supported on an inflatable pillow at the edge of the pool. His face loomed above her, disturbingly close and she shut her eyes quickly.

'That's the idea—relax,' he soothed.

She gasped as his brush moved lower, working steadily over the sensitive curve of her stomach as he massaged the seaweed lotion into her skin. Thank God he was using the brush! But far from relaxing her, he was arousing her to a fever pitch such as she had never experienced before. When the brush came into contact with the soft skin of her inner thighs, she sat up abruptly. 'I . . . I've had enough,' she gasped.

He took in her hectic colouring and wide eyes and rested a hand on her wrist. 'Your pulse is racing,' he commented. 'Perhaps the spa was a little too hot for you.'

She longed to tell him that he was responsible for the fever welling in her but it seemed he was totally unmoved. 'Yes, that's it,' she agreed then became aware of the roguish glint lighting his dark eyes. 'You devil!' she gasped. 'You did that on purpose.'

'Did what?' he asked with studied innocence.

'You know perfectly well. This humility of yours, all this "yes ma'am, no ma'am, three bags full ma'am" is an act, isn't it? You couldn't resist showing me who's really the boss, could you?'

He shrugged. 'I suppose you know what you mean.'

'You bet I do. Get out of here.'

To her chagrin, he went. She had half expected him to defend himself or try to assert his superiority in some other way. And if he had, it would have been no contest, she realised abjectly. Although she was technically the boss, he had made his point more vividly than words could have done. The question was—why had he done it? Was it out of pride? Or did he have some other motive?

Moodily, she swathed herself in a towel and began to blot herself dry. So heightened was the sensitivity of her skin after his treatment that the velour towel could have been made of sandpaper. Every pulse point throbbed and her whole body ached for the fulfilment his stimulation had promised but hadn't delivered. What sort of game was he playing?

A week later, she was no nearer to finding out. She became so caught up with work on Pacific Centre that she had no chance to ask Colleen for more information about his background. Besides which he had behaved impeccably from then on. If it hadn't been for the experience in the spa pool, she would have had no doubts about him.

In the short time he had worked for her, Christopher had become so valuable to her that she wondered how she had ever managed without him.

It wasn't just that the house gleamed with polish and was heady with the scent of fresh flowers and carefully tended plants, or that she was eating like royalty thanks to his gourmet cooking. It wasn't even Bosun's obvious devotion to the newcomer, although the dog was so besotted with Christopher that he didn't even greet Drew at the door any more.

It was something less tangible but it affected her more than anything else. He gave her his time unstintingly.

It was the first time in her life anyone had paid her so much attention, she marvelled as she sipped the martini which had become a pre-dinner ritual. She found herself waiting expectantly for him to announce that dinner was ready because it meant she could look forward to another few hours of his company.

After the first time when she'd had to insist that he share his meals with her, he now ate with her as a matter of course and seemed to enjoy it as much as she did.

At mealtimes, she was able to forget that she had hired him as her 'wife' and just enjoy his company.

When he came to escort her to the table, she knew tonight would be equally pleasant. His first words confirmed it.

'Well, Drew, how was your day?'

Her heart sang at the question. 'When you ask me that, I get the feeling you're not just doing it out of duty—you really want to know.'

'Of course I do.' His expression softened. 'I'm interested in everything about you.'

Eagerly she launched into a summary of the day's progress on Pacific Centre. Now and then Christopher interrupted to ask a pointed question. After one such, she laughed happily. 'It's a godsend, you having a

property background, Christopher. I can talk to you
about my problems knowing you really understand
and aren't just humouring me.'

At once a shadow darkened his even features. 'I've
been meaning to talk to you about that. There's
something I have to tell you. . . .'

The seriousness in his tone alarmed her. For the
first time it occurred to her that there could be some
other reason why he couldn't get work as an architect.
Impulsively, she reached for his hand. 'You're not in
any trouble are you?'

'No, nothing like that,' he said, impatient at the
interruption. 'It's just. . . .' He was interrupted again,
this time by the summons of the phone. With a soft
curse, he rose. 'I'd better see who that is.' A moment
later he returned, his expression grim. 'It's Garth
Dangerfield.'

Bemused and anxious to know what Christopher
was going to confess to her, she went to the phone and
said impatiently, 'Yes Garth, what is it?'

'I'm not interrupting anything, am I?' the other
man said petulantly.

'No, you're . . . oh, you mean Christopher? He . . .
he works for me.'

'His voice sounded familiar. Do I know him?'

'I don't think so. He just came back from overseas.
What did you want to talk to me about?'

Garth's query concerned some figures he needed to
complete a costing he was working out—nothing that
wouldn't have waited until he saw her tomorrow at the
office, she thought as she replaced the phone. From
his none-too-subtle hinting, she realised Garth had
been angling for an invitation to join her. He had
sounded hurt when she didn't take the hint. Garth was
obviously becoming too serious about her, although
she had avoided encouraging him. She would have to

make a decision about him soon if she didn't want his infatuation getting out of hand.

Thoughtfully, she returned to the table but Christopher was on his feet gathering up the dishes. 'What were you going to tell me before Garth interrupted?' she asked.

His mouth tightened into an implacable line. 'It wasn't important,' he said and carried the dishes towards the kitchen.

Now what had she done wrong? She was sure he had been on the verge of sharing a confidence with her but in the time it had taken her to answer the phone, he had changed his mind.

Could he be jealous of Garth? That could only mean he was attracted to her and she found she rather liked this idea. It was too early to consider whether she could be in love with him but she already knew that he made her feel vibrantly alive. He had been able to arouse in her depths of feeling she never experienced before. Maybe that's what she had been missing with Garth, the lack going unrecognised until now. She hugged the thought to herself, wondering what it would be like to be loved by a man like Christopher.

A few minutes later he returned with the coffee things on a tray. There was only one cup. 'Aren't you having any?'

'No, I still have work to do.'

Before he could slip away again she caught at his arm, searching her mind for an excuse to keep him here a little longer. 'Please stay a minute. I need to talk to you about . . . about a party I want to give in . . . in a week's time.'

He took the chair opposite her and waited, his face impassive, while she went on, talking half to herself as she formulated her plans. 'We haven't had a chance to celebrate the award properly yet so I'd like to invite everyone who helped us pull it off. The guest list will be half business, half personal friends.'

'No problem. Just let me know how many guests are expected and I'll plan a menu for you.'

'Oh, you won't have to cook,' she said hastily. 'We'll call in the caterers so all you do is supervise them. Actually, I rather hoped you'd agree to come as a guest yourself, as my escort.'

She held her breath as she waited for his response. This party would be such a golden opportunity to introduce him to her business associates, one of whom might have an opening for him. Besides which, a small voice inside her whispered, she would like her friends to see her on the arm of a man like Christopher Traig. Let Inky Hedges say she was less than a woman then!

To her acute disappointment, he shook his head. 'I'm sorry, but I won't be at your party.'

'Oh, why not?'

'I believe I'm entitled to some time off and I'd like to take it on that night. Since you're having the party catered you won't need my services.'

'I see. You are entitled to some free time of course, and I can't force you to attend a party. . . .'

'Thank you, I'm glad that's settled.' He rose smoothly and disappeared towards the kitchen. This time she made no move to stop him. Wanting her friends to meet him had been part of her reason for holding the party, but maybe that was why he didn't want to come.

Working for her was one thing but being shown off like a prize possession was probably more than his pride could tolerate. She felt ashamed of herself for even considering it and was suddenly glad he had refused.

Still, the vision of herself, radiant on his arm, stayed with her as she sipped her coffee. One day, she told herself. One day soon.

CHAPTER THREE

ALTHOUGH she was disappointed that Christopher wasn't attending the party, Drew appreciated the hard work he put into the preparations. He stage managed the occasion as meticulously as if it was a building project, sketching table decorations, making up shopping lists and drawing up a schedule of tasks to be done so that Drew was left shaking her head in amazement.

'If your architectural talents match your organisational skills, companies should be falling over themselves to hire you,' she marvelled. 'Come to think of it, I might hire you myself.'

'You already did,' he reminded her quietly.

A shadow darkened her light mood and she looked away. Why did he have to remind her of their relationship now, when she had managed to put it out of her mind? She didn't want to think of him in the role of servant, hadn't done so in fact after his first few days with her. Subtly, their relationship had changed into something much more pleasant and informal—as if he were her friend instead of her employee. Certainly, no other man in her life had ever made her feel so . . . cherished, and all without demanding anything from her for himself. 'I don't think of you as hired help,' she said carefully.

His expression hardened. 'But I am. I was supposed to do for you all the things a wife traditionally does for a man, remember? Barring one, of course,' he added.

'But surely a man and wife can be supportive of one

another without either one being superior to the other?'

'Somebody has to make the decisions.'

'Decisions, sure. But can't they be made in consultation?'

To her surprise, his hands balled into fists which he kept rigidly by his sides. 'Nothing, not even a marriage can be run by committee. Somebody has to take the lead.'

And in a real marriage, it would be Christopher Traig, she was certain. She had seen enough of him to know he would enjoy sharing the domestic chores but it would always be on the same terms on which he worked for her—his own.

Tension stretched between them like a piano wire, vibrant with unspoken challenges until she felt a surge of the old rebellion. The need to assert herself returned. 'If you're such a great leader, why do you stay here as a . . . a *househusband*.' She used the term deliberately to provoke him, but was surprised by the ferocity of his response.

'We had an agreement,' he growled. 'I've never welched on an agreement in my life and I don't intend to start now.'

She felt as if she had been stabbed as the pain of his words knifed through her. 'All the ego stroking, the consideration and the kindness you've shown me—was it all out of duty, then?'

He shook his head like a bear ridding itself of a bee. 'I didn't say that.' All at once, he took a step towards her, something dark and unfathomable in his eyes. He took her hand and brought her fingertips to his mouth, bestowing a butterfly kiss on them. 'Drew, I. . . .'

She held her breath. 'Yes, Christopher?'

The expression he turned on her was a mixture of

tenderness and rage, as if he was fighting an internal battle with himself. Her use of his name seemed to help him reach a decision. He dropped her hand and the shuttered look she'd seen on several occasions, returned. 'It's time you were getting ready for your party,' he said flatly. 'I have to get ready for my appointment as well.'

With that he strode out, leaving her staring at her own bemused expression in the dressing-table mirror. A rage to match his welled up inside her. How dare he play cat and mouse with her like this?'

He was hiding something, she was sure—and she was determined to find out what it was. But there wasn't much she could do about it tonight with her guests arriving in less than an hour. She resolved to have it out with him tomorrow.

Whatever he might pretend, Christopher Traig was no household help. She felt sure his strange attitude had something to do with the vicious way he'd admitted that he knew her father. She shivered and pulled her housegown tighter around herself. What if he was here to do her some physical harm?

She had no further chance to dwell on this possibility because the first of her guests would be arriving soon and she couldn't very well greet them in a housegown and slippers.

She shrugged out of the gown and reached for the hanger on which her dress was arrayed. This time Christopher had pressed the gown for her with his usual aplomb.

In defiance of her critics who accused her of lacking femininity, she had decided to wear a Victorian-style petticoat and camisole outfit trimmed with handmade lace around the hemline and across the dropped shoulders. The mid-calf length was exactly right for her unusual height and the revealing neckline emphasised the swanlike proportions of her neck and shoulders.

As she fastened the gold lamé belt around her slender waist and slipped her feet into gold strap sandals, she gave a sigh of satisfaction. Let anyone say she looked other than feminine in *this* outfit! Then she grimaced. The choice of a virginal white dress might lead her critics to draw their own conclusions, but then they would find something to criticise whatever she did. 'The bigger they are. . . .' she murmured to her reflection.

Her hair needed very little attention, which was why she'd had it styled in a dark halo cut short and layered, graduated behind her ears to shape the nape of her neck. All it needed was a vigorous brushing to bring out its natural sheen.

Her face was more of a challenge, since she wore very little make-up at work. This was a special occasion, however. Over a light foundation, she used ginger blusher to deepen the natural sculptured lines of her face, and brushed on a tawny lipstick, finishing with a coat of lip gloss to give her mouth a full, moist look which, she was not unaware, added to the seductive effect she had created.

What would her father have said if he could see her taking such pains over her appearance? Beauty had been well down his list of qualifications, so she had never bothered much over clothes or make-up while he was alive. She wasn't even sure why she was doing it now, unless it was to provoke more of the admiring glances she had caught Christopher giving her. Not that he would be here to see her efforts tonight, she reminded herself.

'Damn!' she said aloud. Maybe her father had been right. Beauty *was* only skin deep, after all, while brains and ability couldn't be faked with powder and paint.

Whatever the motive, she knew she had to make the effort tonight—for herself as much as for Christopher.

A snuffling noise near her feet reminded her that Bosun would have to be confined to the kitchen during the party. Not everyone appreciated his boisterous behaviour as much as she did. 'Sorry, little fellow,' she apologised as she carried him downstairs.

The catering staff sent by Colleen Bell were already hard at work in the kitchen but agreed to keep a weather eye on Bosun during the evening. Drew set him down in his basket, cast an approving eye over the food being prepared, then wandered into the living room to ensure that all was in readiness there.

She was just adding some last minute touches to a flower arrangement when the doorbell chimed.

It was answered by one of the staff hired for the evening and Drew looked up expectantly as the first arrival was shown in. She recoiled when she saw who it was and the smile of welcome froze on her lips.

'Ah, Drew my dear,' he gushed.

'Good evening, Mr Hedges,' she responded, keeping her tone level with an effort. 'I didn't expect to see you here.'

He smiled back, equally tight-lipped. 'I assumed as much, otherwise you'd probably have drunk poison before allowing me in. As it happened, our social columnist whom you *did* invite was too ill to attend— alas.'

She couldn't help herself. 'You sound heartbroken,' she said, her tone heavy with sarcasm.

He raised an eyebrow. 'My, my. Your words wound me. I'm only doing my job, after all.'

'If you mean muckraking, then you do it magnificently,' she shot back.

She was saved further conversation with him by the timely arrival of two more guests. 'Alderman Pierce

and Esme, how nice to see you,' she said sincerely.
The Alderman had been a judge and supporter of the
Dominick entry in the Walter Burley Griffin award.

'Call me Bernard, please,' the Alderman insisted.
'Now the judging is over, I hope we can just be friends.'

'It is a relief to be able to talk to members of the
judging panel without being suspected of coercion,'
Drew laughed. She spent some time with the alderman
and his wife, whom she liked, discussing the
resurgence of the inner city area where Pacific Centre
was being built. It had inspired a number of other
developers to consider the area for their activities, the
alderman told her.

Reluctantly she moved on to spend some time with
each of her other guests. Inky Hedges she studiously
avoided but was aware that he was studying her from
the corner of the terrace where he had set up court. It
was probably just as well that he was here, she
conceded to herself. What he didn't see first hand, he
would have made up anyway. At least this way, his
libellous column would bear some resemblance to fact.

'If looks could kill, that one would.'

She looked up to find Garth Dangerfield at her
elbow, a champagne glass in each hand. She accepted
the one he proffered and sipped it gratefully. 'You
aren't far wrong. I was just wishing Inky Hedges to
hell and gone.'

Garth wagged a forefinger at her with mock
severity. 'Mustn't speak about our Inky like that.
Remember the power of the press.'

'How could I forget? He holds it over my head like a
sword,' she said ruefully. Garth was scanning the
crowd around them. 'Looking for anyone in particular?'

'Your new houseboy. I'm sure I know his voice
from somewhere.'

'He's not my houseboy, he runs the house for me,' she snapped, regretting her tone as soon as she saw Garth's speculative look. 'He's much too old to be called a boy.'

'From his voice, I wouldn't have said he was in his dotage,' he sniffed, sounding unconvinced.

Drew wished she could tell him to mind his own business but she knew his attitude stemmed from his own all-too-obvious interest in her. While she hadn't encouraged him, she hadn't discouraged him either so she couldn't blame him for how he was behaving now.

It was just as well he had misunderstood her comment about Christopher being too old to be called a boy. If he thought his fancied rival was an elderly man, perhaps it would mollify him for the present. It seemed to have that effect, for which Drew was thankful. She had no personal interest in Garth but was depending on him to steer Pacific Centre to a successful conclusion. She couldn't afford to alienate him at this stage. She sighed. Sometimes being a woman was the very devil when it came to coping with temperamental types like Garth.

Determined to avoid further questioning, she murmured an apology to him and made her way to the buffet where she pretended to be making her selection from the wide choice of dishes. She stiffened as Inky Hedges came up behind her and pinned her against the buffet with his considerable bulk. 'Do you mind?' she asked haughtily.

'Sorry, darling, but it is crowded in here,' he explained. The room was crowded but there was no one within feet of Hedges. By now, he was rather the worse for the drinks he had consumed and Drew regarded him with distaste, turning her body deliberately to stone to avoid giving him the slightest satisfaction from the contact.

'I take it you wanted to speak to me,' she queried in the same icy tone.

'I've been wanting to do that all evening, darling, but you've been avoiding me for some reason.'

'Get on with it, can't you?'

'In good time, in good time. I wanted to know what you think of young Monroe, who is now head of your favourite rival company. You know, of course, that dear old Darcy Monroe is flat on his back after his stroke?'

What was he getting at? 'Yes, I'd heard about that,' she said levelly, still pinned beside the buffet by Hedges' body. 'But I haven't met his son since he came home to take over so I can't give you an opinion.'

Hedges' eyes narrowed in disbelief. 'Come on now, Drew. The grapevine is buzzing with the news that you and young Monroe are shacked up together.'

If the idea wasn't so repulsive, she would have laughed in the columnist's face. The idea of her having anything to do with one of the hated Monroes was unthinkable so she smiled her most noncommittal smile—her Mona Lisa look, her father had called it. 'You must be mistaken,' she said with all the coolness she could muster.

'Hardly. My spies are remarkably efficient—as you've found to your cost in the past.'

She ignored this. Hedges was drunk and hoping to draw an indiscreet comment out of her with his outrageous accusations, she decided. 'What do your spies tell you this time?' she asked heavily.

With obvious relish he hesitated then went on. 'They say young Traig Monroe has been living under this very roof for the last month. He's been seen going in and out of here, even driving your car—so there's no point in denying it.'

At the mention of the name of the Monroe heir, she felt the hair on the back of her neck lift slightly. For as long as she could remember, they had been called 'Old Man Monroe' and 'young Monroe'—or 'that Monroe whelp' as her father referred to Darcy Monroe's son. It seemed too great a coincidence that Christopher Traig's surname should be the same as Monroe's first name. Unless Hedges was right and they were one and the same.

Oh, God! Had she been harbouring her rival under her own roof? Christopher Traig, indeed! She had suspected from the first that he was more than he seemed. But she had never considered that he might be a member of the clan which had tried to bring about her own family's downfall.

Hedges watched her intently, but she wasn't going to give him the satisfaction of showing how badly his revelation had upset her. 'Oh, well, it had to come out sometime,' she said with forced lightness.

He looked suspicious. 'You're confirming my story, then?'

'I didn't say that. You . . . you'll read all about it in Dolores Hartman's column before long.'

Hedges blanched. 'You've given her an exclusive?' When she nodded his eyes widened. 'But you know you can't stand that bitch.'

She shrugged. 'Business creates strange bedfellows, Inky.'

He snorted derisively. 'Like you and Monroe. I think there's more to this than you're telling. And even if you have promised the story to la Hartman, you can't stop me digging. It seems too much of a coincidence that the first and second placegetters in the award should suddenly have become bedfellows— to use your quaint expression—after their families have been at daggers drawn for years.'

He paused long enough to take a long pull on his drink but his eyes never left her face. 'Of course you both stand to do very nicely out of the deal, assuming there was a deal. Dominick gets the contract and Monroe gets their cut by invoking the consultant's clause. Am I getting warm?'

'That's the most offensive piece of invention I've ever heard,' she spat at him. 'Get out of here.'

He set his drink down carelessly, spilling some of it on to the Berber carpet. 'Glad to oblige, my dear. I was just about to leave anyway. I've ... er ... got some digging to do.' With an airy wave of his hand towards the other guests, he strode towards the front door. ' 'Bye, darlings. See you all in print.'

After he had gone there was an uneasy silence. Nobody really liked Hedges but they were all forced to tolerate him to avoid reading the worst about themselves in his column. Maggie Symmonds came up to Drew who stood by the buffet, shaking. 'That terrible man,' she clucked sympathetically. 'What was he up to this time?'

Drew smiled wanly at her assistant. 'He's trying to dig up some scandal about the award.'

Maggie grimaced. 'I wish him luck. I've been talking to Bernard Pierce and according to him we won it fair and square. As one of the judges, he ought to know. So Inky can't create a scandal where none exists, can he?'

Drew gave her a grateful smile. 'You're right as usual, Maggie.' Inwardly, she didn't feel so confident. Even an hour ago she would have staked her existence on the integrity of the Dominick entry but until she found out where Traig Monroe fitted into the picture, she couldn't be sure anymore.

The talk resumed again but the party atmosphere had been dispelled by Hedges' departure and one by one the other guests took their leave.

Soon Drew was left alone with the staff who began cleaning away the party debris. While they worked she sat pensively on the couch, nursing but not drinking a glass of champagne.

After the staff left she stayed where she was, unable to summon up enough energy even to go to bed. Besides which she knew she wouldn't get much rest until she'd had some answers from Christopher Traig, or Traig Monroe, whichever he was.

Her mind roved back over the time he had been with her. What had started out as a purely business arrangement, albeit an unusal one, had gradually mellowed into something much more intimate. Against her better judgment she had let herself be beguiled by his thoughtfulness and flattering interest in her. She had started to believe he really cared. Yes, she was forced to admit, she had even fallen a little in love with him.

Her body ached with the memory of his touch when he massaged her in the spa. He intended his touch to be clinical but her response had been the opposite and she was sure he had been more affected than he had let her see. His touch had thrilled her as it had on other occasions when their hands met across a table or their bodies brushed together in passing. He had aroused her as no man had ever done before. Had it all been a ploy to make her vulnerable to him? He must know he had succeeded. But what did he intend to do now?

'Wake up, Drew, you dozed off on the couch.'

She stirred to find the object of her thoughts bending over her. For a minute she had difficulty remembering where she was then it came rushing back and she recoiled from his touch. She must have fallen asleep, exhausted with trying to make sense of Traig Monroe's presence in her house.

With a groan she straightened and automatically

righted the champagne glass which lay on the carpet at her feet.

'Are you feeling all right?' he asked worriedly.

She may as well get it over with. 'I'm perfectly all right, no thanks to you—Traig Monroe.' She watched his face but his expression remained impassive.

'So you know. Good.'

She stared at him. 'Good? Is that all you have to say?'

He dropped down on to the couch and stretched an arm along the back behind her. 'I've been trying to find a way to tell you for quite some time.'

She ignored his arm, resisting the urge to nestle closer into its warm circle. 'Do you really expect me to believe that?'

'Why not? it's the truth.'

'If it is it will be the first one you've spoken since you got here.'

'I guess I deserved that.' Slowly he withdrew his arm and looked down at his hands. 'It would have been so simple if I hadn't started caring about you.'

'The pretence is over so you may as well skip the wifey role now,' she said acidly. 'Tell me one thing. Why did you do it?'

'I wanted to collect evidence to prove that you won the award under false pretenses.'

She laughed bitterly. 'Come on now. We won that fair and square.'

It was his turn to sound bitter. 'Do you call stealing my plans fair and square?'

She felt her face drain of colour. '*What* did you say?'

He uncoiled from the couch and paced towards the glass doors leading on to the terrace, then stood with his back to her. 'I came here to prove that you employed Garth Dangerfield in return for bringing you the plans for my entry,' he said over his shoulder.

She could hardly believe what she was hearing. 'That's crazy!'

'You *do* know that Dangerfield used to work for Monroe's?

'Yes, but. . . .'

'Did he tell you how he got fired?'

'He told me Monroe's son didn't like the way he got along so well with Darcy,' she said.

'Did he also tell you he was taking my father for everything he could, knowing Darcy was too ill to find out?'

This was a different version to the one Garth had told her. 'Obviously he didn't put it like that,' she said, confused.

Traig whirled towards her. 'I'll bet he didn't, but that's the way it happened. I came home on leave and as soon as I realised what was going on I gave him his marching orders. He's lucky I didn't press criminal charges. Now it seems he repaid me for letting him keep his good name by stealing the plans for the Monroe entry which I drew up before I went back to America.'

It was her second massive shock for one evening and it was more than she could take. Her senses reeled. 'I don't believe any of this,' she breathed. 'Get out of my house, out of my life.'

He regarded her steadily. 'I'm afraid you don't get rid of me so easily. You signed a contract with me, remember?'

'No! Colleen Bell signed that.'

'On your delegated authority. What do you think would happen to your reputation if it got around that you reneged on a valid contract?'

Defeated, she rested her head in both hands. 'Why are you doing this?'

'As I said, to find my proof.'

'But why didn't you just come to me with your accusations? We could have talked about it, come to some agreement. . . .'

His smile was wry and humourless. 'Would you have agreed to meet with a Monroe?'

'No.'

'As I thought. Luckily, I was with Colleen Bell hiring some people for Monroe's when you called asking her to find you a wife. I was able to persuade her to put my name down, letting her think it was a harmless joke between us. Incidentally,' he went on when she looked at him in surprise, 'I told her you were in on the whole thing so Colleen isn't to blame.'

No wonder Colleen had taken her request so calmly, Drew thought. She had believed Traig's story that it was a joke. Except that there was nothing funny about how it had turned out. 'What do you plan to do now?' she asked him shakily. 'Will you take your charges to the awards council?'

'It's a bit late for that. They would just treat it as sour grapes. Since Dangerfield took all the copies of my plans when he left I can't prove that they were mine.'

'So you're going to stay here until you get your so-called proof, is that it?' He nodded calmly. Inky Hedges' taunt came back into her mind. Monroe's will get their cut by invoking the consultant's clause, he had said. But before that could happen her company had to run over time or over budget on Pacific Centre. She wouldn't give Monroe that satisfaction! A new idea occurred to her and she raised glittering eyes to him. 'I could go to the council and voluntarily give up the award in favour of Monroe's,' she said.

A gleam of something new and unfathomable came into his eyes. 'That's a solution I hadn't thought of.'

Her worst suspicions were confirmed. 'I'll bet you

hadn't,' she flung at him angrily. 'It's exactly what you were hoping I would do, isn't it? You couldn't win the award fairly so you decided to try trickery instead. Well it isn't going to work, Mr Christoper Traig Monroe—or whatever your name is. You can be my houseboy from now till doomsday and I'll never give in to you.'

'Why don't you ask Garth to confirm or deny what I've said?'

'You'd like that, wouldn't you? You aren't content with destroying my home life. Now you want to start on my love life as well. My father was right—you can't trust a Monroe.'

'That's just great coming from a Dominick who's as two-faced as the rest of her clan. You just proved it by your refusal to confront Dangerfield. It seems you're so besotted with him you're afraid to find out the truth.' He spun around and was halfway to the door before she realised that he was walking out on her.

'Just a minute. Where do you think you're going?'

'Out. Before I do some real damage.'

'We have a contract as you reminded me,' she said icily. 'That means you still work for me and I've just decided you aren't off duty yet.'

His brows came together in an ominous frown and she saw his hands clench and unclench at his sides, then he seemed to reach a decision and shrugged. 'Have it your way. What would you like me to do for you?' His tone was far less accommodating than his words.

She said the first thing which came into her head. 'Start the spa pool.' At once he turned, and soon after she heard him in the pool room. She sank wearily on to the couch, feeling as if she had been physically beaten by the encounter. She really didn't want a bath right now but she felt a strong urge to get even with him. Forcing him into the role of her servant was the best way she could think of at the moment.

How could he let her think he cared about her then let her down like this? And then to accuse her of stealing the plans which won her company the award—she could have tolerated anything but that. Even his version of how Garth Dangerfield came to leave Monroe's was a farce, probably cooked up to further discredit Garth in her eyes.

Her father had been right. The Monroes were nothing but trouble and Traig was as bad as the rest of them. She grabbed one of the cushions and hugged it fiercely then began to pummell it with balled fists. How could he do this to her? Believing he was a struggling out-of-work architect who deserved a break, she had taken him into her home and—yes, she may as well face it, into her heart. It was too cruel.

'If you've finished beating that cushion to a pulp, the pool is ready,' came his voice from the doorway.

With all her might she heaved the cushion towards him but it bounced harmlessly off the jamb and fell at his feet. At least throwing it had relieved some of her pent-up fury. There was no way she was going to do in front of him what she really felt like doing, which was break down and howl like a child. So she rose with all the dignity she could contrive and walked towards him like a queen.

Another thought occurred to her and she turned. He hadn't moved from his position at the side of the door. 'I'd like another massage,' she said haughtily.

Showing no trace of reaction, he merely inclined his head. 'As you wish.'

Rage, frustration and the effects of the champagne she'd consumed at the party were making her reckless, she knew, but she had never felt so driven in all her life. She knew exactly how she was going to exact revenge on him.

She would let him see her, want her, and then make him suffer the torment of the damned knowing that by deceiving her he had put her forever beyond his reach. That it had also put him beyond hers, she wasn't yet ready to face. The impact of that would come later, when she was alone in bed and could give full reign to the despair which was so close to the surface. For now, let him be the one to suffer.

Although he made no sound, she knew he had followed her into the pool room as surely as if he had announced the fact. His very presence set her senses leaping. But she forced herself to appear calm as she turned full-on to him then, ever so slowly, she slid out of her evening gown, pulling it over her head with a deliberately seductive movement. As the fabric went over her head, she heard his indrawn breath and smiled her satisfaction into the folds of the garment. Her bra was next to go, leaving only her the fragile lace panties around her hips. She wished she had the nerve to slip them off as well but courage deserted her and she turned her back to him to remove them, then slid quickly into the steaming spa bath.

'My shoulders and back first,' she instructed when he came up behind her, the massage lotion in one hand.

The heat his hands radiated made her flinch as he obediently began to work the lotion into her shoulders. His breathing was laboured, the sounds rasping in his throat as if he was fighting for control of himself. 'Is something the matter?' she asked silkily.

His grip tightened on her shoulder. 'You know damn well there is. You think you've found a way to get even with me, don't you?'

'Haven't I?'

'Maybe. On the other hand, you could be pushing your luck.'

'What's that supposed to mean?' she asked, although she was afraid she already knew his answer.

'It means I could take you right here, now, in the pool—and you couldn't do a damn thing to stop me.'

'But you wouldn't.'

He stood up abruptly, dropping the lotion so the plastic bottle clattered on to the slate tiled surround. 'No, I wouldn't. Whatever you think you know about me, I'm no rapist. But I *am* human. So I suggest you get out of there and put some clothes on while I still have some self-control left. Then you and I have to talk.'

'Talk about what?' she asked, but she was talking to empty air. He had already gone. Resignedly, she stepped out of the spa and reached for a bath sheet, swathing it around herself. What could he have to say to her?

Earlier, he said he intended to come clean about who he really was. He had also said he cared about her. Could it possibly be true that his consideration *hadn't* all been an act—that he had begun to feel the same way she did? The idea thrilled her but she couldn't dismiss the fact that he was a Monroe. Nothing in her upbringing allowed for any softening towards them. And yet. . . .

Without warning, the room tilted crazily around her and she clutched at the towel rail to steady herself. It must be the combined effects of the champagne and the too-warm spa which were making her feel so faint. Or else it was the strain of trying to sort out her feelings towards Traig Monroe . . . or Christopher. She still didn't know which it was. Heavens, she did feel peculiar. The floor began to swim beneath her feet, as if the tiles had turned liquid. Really alarmed now, she staggered towards the door, afraid that if she collapsed here she would end up head first in the spa pool.

'Christopher!' she called shakily, then called again more urgently. Where was he? And why were the lights dimming and brightening so dizzily?

Then everything turned to velvet blackness and she gave herself up to it gratefully.

CHAPTER FOUR

'DREW, can you hear me?'

Reluctantly she struggled out of her cocoon of blackness and opened her eyes, closing them again with a groan of protest as light dazzled her. Instead of the hard floor of the spa there was the softness of her own bed beneath her. But how had she got here?

'You fainted,' a rasping male voice supplied. She opened her eyes again to find Monroe standing at her bedside, his anger now supplanted by concern for her. When he saw that she was looking at him, he frowned. 'You silly fool. You shouldn't have gone into the spa after drinking all that champagne.'

She remembered now. Earlier, he had found her with an upturned champagne glass at her feet. He must think she had been drinking heavily. 'I only had a couple of glasses,' she insisted.

'Are you sure?'

'Of course I'm sure.'

'Then I'm glad I took the precaution of calling Doctor Davis. I found his number in your address book.'

She struggled to sit up then made a grab for the bedclothes as she realised she was naked under them, although it was a bit late for that since he must have carried her in here like this. 'There was no need for a doctor, I'm fine, really.'

'Practising medicine without a licence again, Drew?' Alan Davis, the Dominicks' long-time family physician and friend came into the room and dropped his black bag on to her bed. 'Your friend here tells me you passed out for no good reason. That's always cause for concern.'

She darted an anxious look at Christopher. The doctor referred to him as her 'friend', showing no signs of surprise that a strange man should have been the one who found her after she fainted in her bath in the small hours of the morning. It must be commonly accepted that she and Monroe were living together. She should have realised the impression having a single man living under her roof would create. But it was too late to undo the damage now. There would be time enough to worry about such things when she felt better.

Doctor Davis eyed her with concern. 'How long have you been feeling off-colour?'

'I haven't . . .' she began, then decided she had better be honest with him if he was to help her, 'I haven't felt really well for ages. But it's only in the last few days that everything was getting on top of me. The slightest effort seemed almost too much trouble.'

'How long is it since you took a holiday?'

Her answering laugh was tinged with bitterness. 'Since Dad died, I haven't had time to even think about holidays. Then there was the lead-up to the award. . . .'

'Just as I thought,' the doctor interrupted, 'you've let yourself get run down. Tonight's episode was a warning that if you keep it up you're heading for a complete breakdown.'

While she assimilated this disturbing news, the doctor shooed Traig Monroe out of the bedroom then insisted on giving her a complete check-up. At last, he slipped his stethoscope out of his ears.

'Will I live?' she asked cheekily, sounding more confident than she felt. She had never had a serious illness in her life and the prospect frightened her.

'There's nothing wrong with you that a spell of relaxation won't fix,' he told her. 'I'd like you to make arrangements to go away at once—tomorrow if you can.'

'Oh, but, I can't leave the business!' she protested.

'If I can, why can't you?' Monroe asked, coming back into the room. He sat down on the edge of her bed. 'I know you think the company will fall apart if you're not at the helm—my father thought that, too.'

'So did mine,' she said soberly, understanding what he was driving at. 'But both organisations had to carry on without them in the end, didn't they?'

'My point exactly. When do we leave?'

She stared at him. 'Wait a minute, you aren't going anywhere.'

'She'll need someone to take care of her, won't she, Doctor?' Alan Davis nodded agreement. 'There, see, doctor's orders.'

'Men! You all stick together,' she fumed, then gestured significantly at the doctor. 'You know why we can't go away together,' she hissed at Traig.

Monroe shrugged, ignoring her warning gesture. 'Why not? Everybody already thinks we're an item.'

She slumped back against the pillows. What was the use? Having wormed his way into her life, Traig Monroe was determined to haunt her every waking minute with his absurd accusations that she had stolen his entry in the award.

On the other hand, if he was with her, he couldn't do anything to sabotage the progress of Pacific Centre. A smile of devilment tilted up the corners of her mouth. 'Very well, then—have it your way,' she told the doctor with mock resignation. 'I'll take a holiday and he can come along to look after me.'

'That's the spirit,' the doctor smiled. He gathered

up his things and started towards the door, saying he would like to see her again when she got back from her rest cure.

When he had gone, Monroe looked at her suspiciously. 'You gave in much too easily just now. What are you up to?'

'What makes you think I'm up to anything?'

'I have a suspicious mind. Where did you plan on taking your cure—some rich resort with a telex and a landline to your office?'

She shook her head. 'I'm going to be good for once and do just as the doctor ordered. I know just the place for it.'

Three days later, they were flying high over the weather in the air-conditioned comfort of a Beechcraft executive prop jet. Drew had handed over the co-ordination of Pacific Centre to Garth Dangerfield, and the management of the office to a stunned Maggie Symmonds, who also agreed to mind Bosun while his owner was away. Maggie had rolled her eyes in amazement when she found out who Drew's travelling companion was to be.

'Traig Monroe—how could you?' she moaned.

'Don't tell me that Dad would turn over in his grave—I somehow think he'd approve of what I'm doing.'

Despite everything, she really believed it. While he had no love at all for the Monroes, her father had always encouraged her to do what she believed was right. In his own awkward way, he had wanted her to be happy and if teaming up with a Monroe would achieve that, he would have told her to go right ahead. He may not have been pleased but he would have understood, she felt sure.

Now, as they winged their way across the South

Pacific, she stole a glance at her travelling companion. The sight of him sprawled comfortably in the armchair-like seat set her pulses racing. He had insisted on going along to pay her back for stealing his plans, she was sure, but she had her own reasons for wanting him with her and, so far, she hadn't dared to explore fully what they might be. She was more strongly attracted to him than she had ever been to any man in her life and she wanted to explore where the attraction might lead. Alone with him, she would have the chance—if she could only manage to convince him that his charges were absurd and totally unfounded.

'You still haven't told me our precise destination,' he said, breaking into her thoughts.

'That's because I wasn't sure you'd agree to come if you knew it's name,' she said mischievously.

'Well you'll have to tell me soon.'

She took a deep breath. 'Honeymoon Island.'

'I can see that nervous exhaustion hasn't affected your sense of humour,' he said dryly. 'But it isn't my opinion you should worry about. What does Garth Dangerfield think about you heading for somewhere called Honeymoon Island with me?'

Traig obviously believed there was something between herself and Garth, using as evidence her refusal to confront him with Traig's accusations. Until she did that, Traig would never accept that she and Garth were mere business associates. Yet if she confronted Garth on Traig's say-so and he turned out to be wrong, Garth would be justified in walking out on Pacific Centre—then where would she be?

'But what if the plans really *were* stolen?' a small voice in her head argued. No, it couldn't be true. Because if they were, she was as guilty as Garth for accepting them at face value. If the truth was made public, Dominick's reputation and her own would be in shreds and the company her father had left in her care would be badly damaged. Was that the real reason for her refusal to investigate Traig's charges—the fear that he might be right, and that she would be unable to live up to her father's expectations for her? Unhappily, she rested her head in her hands.

'Are you feeling all right?' Traig asked worriedly.

'Yes, terrific,' she responded bleakly .

'You still didn't tell me what Garth thought of you going away with me.'

'I didn't tell him. I mean, he knows I'm going away to have a rest but not that you are with me.'

'I see,' he said, tight-lipped.

No, you don't see at all, she wanted to cry out but she kept silent. She would have a better chance of making him see her point of view once they were alone on the island.

Honeymoon Island had been her father's wedding present to her mother and gained its name because her parents had spent the first weeks of their married life on the island. It was a slim crescent of land only five kilometres long and was located near the resort island of Lord Howe, about two hours flying time from Sydney.

The island was the exposed part of a long-dead volcano which erupted out of the sea in pre-history. Its flanks were cloaked in luxuriant palm forests and a dozen secluded beaches ringed the low-lying foreshores. Remote from the world's shipping lanes and with no safe anchorage for large vessels, it had remained virtually undisturbed until it was bought by a reclusive artist known only as Trader George. When he retired to the mainland, he sold the little island to Andrew Dominick and it became the family's retreat from the world.

Although Andrew's visits had been clouded by the island's association with the beloved wife he had lost in childbirth, he used to say he found more peace here than anywhere else on earth.

To Drew, the island had no such unhappy associations. She remembered it only as the carefree playground of her childhood where everything was coloured turquoise and gold and the air was alive with tropical scents and fluorescent-hued butterflies.

She could hardly wait to get out of the plane and breathe the fragrant air.

'You really love this place, don't you?' Traig observed as he watched her spread her arms wide as if receiving a benediction.

'It feels more like home than Sydney ever does.'

The elderly caretaker whom Drew introduced to Traig as Oliver Daintree, collected their luggage from the plane and loaded it on to a motorised cart which was the only four-wheeled transportation on the island. In the ungainly vehicle they set off towards a cluster of cottages set on a rise above the main lagoon.

'It's good to have you back, Miss Dominick,' Oliver Daintree said with a touch of censure in his tone.

'I know, I've left it far too long,' she agreed. 'Looking at this place, I can't imagine why.'

They were deposited outside a long, low building which had a wide front verandah overlooking the lagoon. Daintree stopped only long enough to unload their cases and set them down on the verandah then he climbed back into the vehicle.

'Doesn't he live in one of these buildings?' Traig asked.

Drew shook her head. 'Oliver's a bit of a hermit. He has a cabin on the other side of the island. We probably won't see him again until we're ready to leave.'

'How will he know when we want to go?'

'Telephone, silly. The island isn't as primitive as it looks—but there are no telex machines, promise!' she added, catching his suspicious look.

'Then what are the other buildings used for?'

'Guest accommodation. Dad used to bring a favoured few business associates here for conferences.'

'How many people are on the island now?'

Unaccountably nervous, she ran her tongue along her full lips, moistening them before she answered. 'Nobody. Apart from Oliver, there isn't another soul on the island.'

To her chagrin, he seemed more annoyed than titillated by the idea. 'Didn't I warn you about pushing your luck?' he growled.

He picked up their cases as if they weighed nothing then shouldered open the flyscreen door and went inside, leaving her no choice but to follow meekly in his wake. He seemed determined to keep up the barriers between them. Was he so convinced of her guilt that he wouldn't permit himself any other feelings towards her? She knew he found her desirable so the problem had to be that he didn't choose to see her as other than a rival. She sighed deeply. Everything had been so promising when she believed he was Christopher Traig, unemployed architect. Why did he have to change back into Traig Monroe and set his vile accusations up as a barrier between them?

He had placed her luggage in the master bedroom which had belonged to her parents, she found when she went inside.

The queen-size bed, obviously meant for two, mocked her, so she turned her back on it and went to the shuttered French windows which opened on to the verandah, flinging them wide to let the afternoon sunshine stream into the room.

The view was breathtaking from the hibiscus and frangipani trees and coconut palms among which the cottage nestled, to the wide stretch of shimmering sand only yards away. Its peace enveloped her until she started to believe that it wouldn't be long before she convinced Traig of her innocence and left him free to ... to do what? To love her? Was that what she wanted? 'Yes, yes,' her heart answered.

He had chosen the single room which was separated from hers by a shared bathroom. She had often slept in the single room herself while her father used the larger one. Often, they had visited one another by taking a shortcut through the bathroom. She wondered if Traig would do that. Timidly, she opened her door but the door which opened on to Traig's room remained firmly closed so she retreated to her own room and started unpacking.

It wasn't long before she had her clothes neatly stowed away and she could explore the rest of the house. Everything was just as she remembered it, from the white-painted cane furniture with its gay floral printed covers, to the woven rattan wall-hangings her father had collected on his trips to the South Seas. Oliver had stocked the kitchen cupboards with enough tinned and packaged food to feed an army and there was fresh cream, bananas and citrus fruit from the tiny farm he ran on the other side of the island.

'Where does all this stuff come from?' Traig asked, coming in behind her.

'Oliver brings the packaged goods over by boat from Lord Howe Island,' she explained and went on to tell him about the small farm. 'As a child, I thought that all the fruit and dairy produce was left by a good fairy,' she told him. 'One day I got up at dawn, determined to catch our generous spirit. I was terribly disappointed to find it was only Oliver.'

'And I thought I was your first big disappointment in life,' Traig said thoughtfully.

She was reluctant to spoil the pleasant mood. 'Must we talk about that?'

He frowned in concern. 'Not if you're tired. You are here to recuperate, after all. Would you like to rest while I organise dinner?'

'I'm glad you didn't suggest doing things the other way around,' she smiled, amusement making her forget for a moment all that stood between them.

'You couldn't be as bad a cook as all that?' he teased, responding to her mood.

'Worse! I can manage an omelette and a Chef's salad but that's about it. Unless you count sandwiches—I'm sensational at those.'

He rolled his eyes in mock dismay. 'I knew there was a good reason why you agreed to bring me along. Out of the cook's way then, and have your rest. I'll call you when everything's ready.'

Tugging at a non-existent forelock, she backed out of the kitchen, hearing his laughter follow her. Then there was silence, followed by the purposeful clatter of saucepans as he started to prepare their meal. She made her way out to the verandah and stretched full length on a cane chaise longue which was angled to provide an uninterrupted view of the lagoon.

The journey had tired her, she discovered to her surprise. She was so used to having unlimited reserves of energy that it came as a shock to discover she had the same limitations as other people. She had always been the one who could work until midnight and keep a breakfast appointment next day without turning a hair. Which was why she was in her present run-down condition, she supposed.

She stirred restlessly on the longue. What was the matter with her? She was usually so confident and self-assured. Could this confused, hypersensitive state she was in now possibly be love, or was it only a by-product of her exhaustion? She dismissed the disturbing question from her mind and concentrated instead on soaking up the hot sun, redolent with the perfume of frangipani. Her last waking thought was that someone must have slipped lotus blossoms into the glass of champagne she had drunk on the plane.

'Wake up, sleepyhead, dinner's almost ready.'

She stretched luxuriantly. 'I must have drifted off.'

Her eyes met his and her senses leapt at the sight of him, lithe and tanned, as if his skin was already responding to the island sun. He had changed into an open-necked Hawaiian shirt which skimmed the athletic lines of his body. Faded blue jeans fitted low around his hips, emphasising his lean build and making her disturbingly aware of how masculine he was.

She didn't tell him that her dreams had been of running along the golden sand with him, then of lying with him at the water's edge, their bodies entwined. Hot colour suffused her skin as the details came rushing back. She pushed the thoughts away and stood up. 'Do I have time to change clothes before dinner?'

'It's a cold meal so take as long as you like.'

Thankfully, she fled to her own room and stood for a long time under an icy shower which left her skin tingling. Then she dressed in a halter-necked sundress which showed off her smooth shoulders and back. On impulse, she reached out of her window and snapped off a scarlet hibiscus blossom which she tucked into her hair above her left ear. In some island cultures, the side on which you wore the blossom indicated whether or not you were interested in a man. Trouble was, she couldn't remember which ear conveyed which message. Oh, well, Traig would just have to put his own interpretation on the location of the flower.

He whistled appreciatively when he saw her, and rose to pull out her chair. 'Drew, you are unquestionably the most beautiful woman on this island.'

'Flatterer,' she demurred, but was pleased, nonetheless.

Despite the fact that most of the ingredients had come out of tins or packets, Traig had performed miracles in the kitchen. They started with avocadoes stuffed with crabmeat, followed by prawns and a rice salad, and an intoxicating dessert of bananas soaked in brandy and flamed at the table, then doused with thick cream. To her disgust, Drew finished off every morsel. 'I didn't realise I'd acquired such an appetite,' she said apologetically.

He raised his wine glass in salute. 'Here's to your appetite.'

She flushed, unsure whether he meant for food or—something else.

They shared the task of clearing up and washing the dishes and Drew found the activity curiously satisfying. 'This is what it would be like if we were married,' she caught herself thinking and froze in the act of putting away the plates. It was the first time she had ever thought of marriage in relation to herself. She had always been too wrapped up in the company and in any case, would never have considered deserting her father while he needed her. That restraint no longer applied but there was still the company to think about—and the fact that Traig was a Monroe. However attracted to him she was, he was still her family's enemy and worse, one who believed her capable of industrial theft.

'Let's have our coffee and liqueurs out on the verandah,' he suggested, not sounding much like an enemy at all.

They sat together in companionable silence, letting the island's peace wash over them as they watched the eternal spectacle of the sun setting over the lagoon. After a few minutes, Drew glanced at Traig. 'Who's running things at Monroe's while you're here?'

'I thought the idea was to get away from business?'

'It is. But I'm still curious.'

'Very well. I have a very capable second-in-command. I don't ever want to be a one-man-band like Dad.'

Or my father and now me, Drew thought uncomfortably. Aloud, she said, 'How is your father?'

'He's very restricted in what he can do for himself. The doctors hold out a little hope that he'll recover, although he may linger in his present state for months.'

'I'm surprised you didn't want to stay in Sydney to be near him.'

'There's nothing I can do there. The doctors promised to contact me here if I'm needed, but they thought it was safe for me to leave. Dad doesn't recognise me at the moment, although that may change. He may even get some movement back. It's really in the lap of the gods now.'

'How terrible for you,' she breathed, thinking how merciful it had been that her father had gone quickly. There had been no warning. One heart attack and it was all over. 'My father would have hated to linger like that.'

'That's the worst of it, we don't know what Dad is thinking and feeling because he can't tell us.' Traig's voice caught and he tailed off.

He really cares, Drew thought, touched. Reflexively, she reached across and caught his hand, feeling his fingers tighten convulsively around hers. To distract him from his painful thoughts, she asked, 'What made you pick Christopher for an alias?'

'Because it's my name.'

'But I thought. . . .'

'I know. I was named Christopher Traig Monroe after my grandfather. To avoid confusion between us, I was known by my middle name.'

'I liked Christopher, you know.'

'Then what's so hard to take about Traig?'

She hesitated. 'Christopher didn't accuse me of stealing the award-winning plans, unlike Traig.'

'That's because Christopher let himself be blinded by your charms,' he said with an edge of bitterness in his tone. 'Christopher managed to convince himself that you couldn't possibly be in league with Garth Dangerfield but when you refused to confront Garth, it was left to Traig to draw his own conclusions.'

'It's as if we're both two people in one,' she observed painfully. 'Traig is as different from Christopher as . . .'

'. . . as Drew is from Miss Dominick, company director,' he finished for her.

'We could leave the other two behind while we're here,' she suggested gently.

'Yes, we could.'

He had retained his grip on her hand and now he pulled her out of her chair, towards him until she was drawn on to his lap. Of their own accord, her arms went around his neck and she rested her head against his chest. Under her cheek she could feel the rapid-fire pounding of his heart.

Then he reached under her chin and tilted her face up to his. In the half-darkness his lips found hers, the soft bristle of his moustache stroking her upper lip in a disturbingly sensual action. The urgency of his kiss told her he had been wanting this moment as much as she had. His mouth against hers was fiercely demanding, his tongue flicking insistently against her lips until she parted them to let him explore the inside of her mouth.

An explosion of feeling surged through the far reaches of her body and she pulled back in alarm. 'My god, what was that?'

'Leave the company director out of this,' he growled. 'Drew doesn't ask stupid questions.'

What Drew did was to return kiss for kiss with a passion which mounted to almost unbearable heights. His body pressed against hers, closer and closer as if her clothes, sheer though they were, were more of a barrier between them than he could stand. At last, he stood up, holding her against him. 'Let's go inside.'

She experienced a moment of panic. Was this what she really wanted? With blinding clarity, she knew that it was. She ached for the fulfilment of his possession more than she had ever wanted anything in her life before. The company director with her instinct for self-censorship had fled. So too, it seemed, had Traig Monroe and his suspicions. That left only Drew and Christopher and their driving need for each other.

In the bedroom, the huge bed which had mocked her solitary state now seemed barely large enough to contain their combined excitement.

Her eyes remained locked with his as they impatiently dispensed with their clothes. Never before had such a tide of emotion swept through her.

She was a child again, waiting for the ice cream van whose enticing bell she could hear a block away. She was a teenager pacing up and down the hall as she waited for her first grown-up date to arrive.

Then she was a woman in his arms, their bodies fitting together like two pieces of a puzzle as they soared together towards the sweetly tormenting pinnacle for which the child and the teenager had been innocently rehearsing.

Much later, she stroked a finger down the hard column of his spine. 'I'm glad we got rid of the other man, the one with the suspicious mind,' she said teasingly.

'This one has a suspicious mind, too,' he said, surprising her by taking her comment seriously. Surely he wasn't going to bring the award up *now*? Instead, he went on, 'I know that tonight was something new for you, so where did you learn to behave so . . . so provocatively?'

She hadn't been able to conceal from him the fact that she had never fully shared herself with a man before, but everything else had been pure instinct. 'I had a good teacher,' she confessed, hugging him to show him whom she meant.

To her astonishment, he tautened in her arms and rolled away so his back was turned to her. 'I see,' was all he said.

Surely he didn't think anyone else had been her teacher! She must be imagining the sudden coldness between them. But before she could ask him to explain his breathing became deep and even, indicating that he was asleep.

The single room was never used after that night. By mutual consent, Traig moved his belongings into the master bedroom and Drew gladly made room for them in the vast built-in wardrobe. She soon forgot his odd behaviour of that first night in her new-found euphoria and the new arrangements seemed to set the seal on their happiness.

'Enjoying yourself?' he asked a few nights later as they sat sipping their coffee on the verandah. With no radio or television to distract them, it had become their habit to spend the evenings talking and dreaming like this.

'Silly question,' she smiled. 'Aren't you?'

'It can't last you know,' he observed sombrely. 'Traig and Miss Dominick will be back.'

'But not yet? Please?' Relieved when he inclined his head in agreement, she relaxed 'But speaking of those two, it's good to know that everything is going along smoothly at the office.'

He glanced at her sharply. 'What makes you so sure?'

'Simple process of deduction. They haven't called with any problems, therefore everything must be going well.' She sighed contentedly. 'It's been heavenly having this week to myself. I hadn't realised how much the business was running my life.'

'Isn't that up to you?'

She grimaced. 'In theory, yes. But it was hard enough getting the management of Dominick's to accept a woman at the helm, far less someone my age. I've had to work harder and longer than anyone else, just to prove I'm as good as they are.'

'Is it so important?'

'I feel I owe it to my father. He built the company from nothing and since he didn't have a son to carry on, I had to. There wasn't any choice really.'

'Yes, there was. You could have gone right away, somewhere your name didn't mean anything, where you would have to stand or fall on your own merits.'

'Is that what you did?'

'It's what I tried to do. I was forced to come home after Dad first became ill but he wouldn't let anyone tell him how to do anything so I went away again. Then he had the stroke and I had to come back.'

'The one-man band?' she mused, remembering his earlier use of the phrase.

'Exactly. When he collapsed completely, it was almost impossible for anyone to take over the reins. I vowed then that I'd never be like that.'

The music of the cicadas singing in the forest rose to such a crescendo that further talk was drowned out and they sat back, sipping their drinks and immersing themselves in the hypnotic sound.

Drew shivered slightly and stood up. 'I'm going inside to get a wrap.'

Luckily, she'd packed a hand-crocheted wool shawl which was perfect for draping around her shoulders after the sun's warmth left the island. She went to fetch it and was standing at the open wardrobe door, foolishly delighting in the sight of his clothes nestling alongside hers, when an unexpected sound mingled with that of the cicadas. Then it stopped. She shrugged the shawl on and returned to the verandah just as Traig was also emerging from the house.

'Was that the telephone?' she asked.

'Yes, it was,' he confirmed.

'Oh?' She waited for him to tell her who the caller was but since he remained silent, she went on, 'who was it?'

He hesitated for the merest moment. 'It was for me—business.'

'No problems, I hope?'

'No. No problems.'

Relieved, she accepted his statement at face value. It was only later, as she lay beside him in the enormous bed, that she remembered that Traig hadn't known that the island possessed a telephone until she'd told him about it. How could his associates have known where to call him?

'Traig,' she said suddenly, 'did you phone your office and give them this number?'

'What? Oh ... of course,' he confirmed, sounding edgy. She wished it wasn't so dark that was unable to read his expression.

She should have known he would call his office to let them know where he was, so there was nothing untoward about the phone call. Nevertheless, the uneasy feeling persisted and it was a long before she fell into a troubled sleep.

CHAPTER FIVE

IN the golden light of a new day her suspicions seemed incredibly childish and she was tempted to tell him what she had been thinking. But afraid of spoiling the rapport which had grown up between them, she said nothing.

'What do you want to do today?' he asked after they had finished one of his sumptuous breakfasts.

'We could go exploring,' she suggested. 'I haven't been all over the island since I was a child. We could take a picnic and have it on whichever of the beaches is the most sheltered from the wind today. I'll even provide the lunch, since you've done all the cooking so far.'

'In that case, you're on,' he agreed.

She was already as dressed as she needed to be, in a wine print bandeau bikini with a matching skirt tied around the waist and her feet slipped into raffia sandals. He was dressed more conservatively, so while he went to change she disappeared into the kitchen to deliver on her promise.

It would have to be sandwiches, of course, since her other party piece, an omelette, would hardly do for a beach picnic. Her famous Chef's salad was suitable to carry so she arranged the ingredients in an airtight plastic container.

The sandwiches she made from alternating slices of brown and white bread, filled with layers of canned ham and asparagus spears then cut into finger-width ribbons. Proud of her handiwork, she swathed the sandwiches in clear plastic wrap and piled them into a

wicker basket with the salad, adding plump yellow
bananas for dessert and a flask of chilled white wine to
wash it all down.

'Quite a feast for someone who says she can't cook,'
Traig commented, coming into the kitchen. He had
changed into hip-hugging yellow swim shorts and a
floral print shirt left open to reveal his tanned chest.

'I don't know whether we'll need the food after all,'
she laughed. 'Dressed like that, you look good enough
to eat.'

'I'm glad you approve.'

She squealed when he pulled her against him so her
exposed midriff was teased by the coarse mat of his
chest hair. As she smiled up at him, he dropped the
lightest of kisses on her parted lips then brushed her
hair back from her face in such a sensuous gesture that
she felt as if she had been made passionate love to,
right here in the kitchen. She couldn't recall when she
had last felt so happy and carefree.

'We don't have to go out, you know,' she said
huskily.

He held her at arm's length. 'Good grief! A week on
this desert island and you've turned into a shameless
wanton.'

It was exactly what she *had* turned into, she realised
with a sense of wonder. But only where he was
concerned. Somehow, they had achieved the miracle
of leaving Traig Monroe and Miss Dominick back on
the mainland. If only they could stay like this once
they were married!

For she was sure it was only a matter of time before
he proposed. He might do it here, on the island, which
was certainly a setting for romance. They belonged
together, that much she knew. If they could only hang
on to that belief long enough to resolve the differences
which existed between them—or rather, between the

two people they would have to turn back into when they returned home.

For the present, those differences had ceased to matter. After a gentle walk through rich vegetation, they emerged on to a secluded beach at the southernmost end of the island. It was ringed by majestic cliffs which dropped sheer into the ocean. Out in the bay, rocks barely washed by the swell of the sea, were alive with birds and the air was filled with their piercing cries.

The profile of the island changed constantly as they walked, as it disclosed new peaks and valleys from each different viewpoint.

'It's hard to believe we have this all to ourselves,' she marvelled as they emerged on to yet another golden beach, innocent of any human footprints.

'Aren't you forgetting Oliver?'

'If I know Oliver Daintree, he's out on the reef, fishing by now.'

'So we really do have the place to ourselves,' he said, his eyes clouding with unmistakable desire. Without saying a word, he dropped the picnic basket to the sand and opened his arms to her. Willingly, she went into them and they sank on to the sun-warmed sand, their bodies creating a shallow well as they burrowed closer together.

While his mouth was busy on hers, he reached behind her and loosened the narrow band of fabric which bound her breasts. Unrestrained, they pressed against him and she felt her nipples harden in response. Her hands roved around under his shirt, revelling in the hard, sculptured feel of him. When he took first one breast, then the other into his mouth, probing the sensitive nipples with his teeth, her breath came in shuddering gasps but she made no move to stop him.

She was his and she wanted him to know it. She welcomed his hands caressing her bare midriff, and exploring inside the band of her wraparound skirt. He tugged at the tie and the skirt fell away, revealing the skimpy bikini briefs. They were also fastened by ties at each side and she held her breath as he tugged those away, too, so she lay in his arms, the golden sand her only covering.

'You are so beautiful,' he breathed.

It was her turn to show him how she felt and again, instinct was her teacher. She pushed him gently back on to the sand and slid the shirt off his shoulders so she could caress his back and chest with firm, knowing strokes. He had to help her ease the swim trunks off but then he lay passively under her exploring hands as she taught herself to know every contour of his body, like a blind person discovering a statue.

Finally, he could stand it no longer as the state of his excitement outpaced his iron control and he rolled over, taking her with him into the well of sand. Soon her throaty cries of pleasure mingled with the calls of the sea birds and the crashing of the waves against the rocks nearby.

Afterwards, he rolled up on to one elbow and studied her, his eyes warm and loving. 'I'm glad you've stopped asking questions,' he teased.

'The company director does that, not me.' She turned over on to her stomach to let the sun warm her back. 'You know, I had a dream about this,' she confessed.

He pretended to be shocked. 'You brazen creature! I thought I was the one making the running and now I find that you planned this all along.'

'That does it!' Laughing, she sat up and pelted him with a handful of sand. Naturally, he returned her fire until they were both covered in sand.

'I think we'd better have a swim, don't you?' Drew gasped, spitting gritty sand out of her mouth.

'Race you to the water.'

It was hardly a contest since the waves were almost at their feet, the tide having crept up on them as they lay together. Gladly, they swooped into the blue-green waves and let the water wash the sand out of their hair. It was the first time she had swum naked in her life and it was a revelation to feel the tingling surf pounding against her unprotected body. A swimsuit would never feel as appealing again.

She gasped as Traig came up from underneath her and pulled her slippery body against him while he kissed her soundly. Then he led her, dripping, from the water to drop down on their towels out of reach of the rising tide.

Mere food was an anti-climax after that but they enjoyed the picnic nevertheless. The wine had stayed chilled in its vacuum flask, and tasted blissful to their heated palates. Drew raised her glass to him. 'To us,' she proposed.

He hesitated for a heartbeat, then raised his own glass in response. 'To Drew and Christopher,' he amended.

It wasn't quite the toast she had proposed but she told herself she was being unnecessarily fussy. Still, the worry persisted and she set her glass down on the sand. 'Traig, do you love me?' she asked tensely.

'Haven't I been demonstrating it ever since we got here?'

'Yes, but do you love *me*—all of me? The company director is still here, inside the beachcomber, you know.'

'I know,' he said heavily. 'I'm not really sure how I feel about her yet. I've been trying to keep her from intruding on us.'

She looked at him sharply. 'What do you mean by that?'

'Just a figure of speech. I meant I've been trying to forget about her, that's all.'

Instinctively, she knew that wasn't all and it was as if the sun had gone in on her day. She stood up and began shaking sand from the towel. 'I think we should go back.'

'It is getting late,' he agreed.

'No, I mean back to the mainland. I've recovered from my exhaustion so there's really no reason to stay here.' And there was every reason to go back, she thought. Her involvement with Traig had grown deeper and more serious than she had allowed for. For her own sake, it was time she found out whether he loved all of her—or just the carefree, compliant spirit who inhabited this island. Moodily, she tied her bikini in place and wrapped the skirt around her waist, then gathered up the picnic things. As soon as Traig was ready, they set off back towards the house.

It was late afternoon by the time they reached it and the lengthening shadows around the house seemed to echo Drew's serious mood. Something had happened to eclipse the sun of their day. The trouble was, she didn't know when or how it had happened. It had started when she reminded him that she was also the company director he disliked, she decided. Surely he wasn't going to turn out to be one of those men who refused to accept that a woman could have as many facets—career and personal—as a man?

'Do you object to a woman having a career?' she asked as they trudged the last few yards towards the house.

He raised a startled eyebrow. 'Good lord no! Why should I?'

'Just wondering.' There was no mistaking the

sincerity of his denial, so if it wasn't her commitment
to her career which was bothering him, then what was
it? There was only the absurd business of the award
entry and surely after the last few days, he knew
enough about her to realise she wasn't capable of such
underhand behaviour? She sighed in frustration. She
had hoped being alone with him on the island would
have helped them to reach an understanding. It
seemed they had, but only between Drew and
Christopher, not between Traig and Miss Dominick.

'You can have the bathroom first,' he offered as
soon as they were inside.

He headed towards the kitchen with the picnic
basket and she escaped from his disturbing presence
into the solitude of the bathroom. Under the needle-
like spray of lukewarm water, she was at least able to
think about him without being distracted by his
physical presence.

There was only one way to resolve the situation
between them. That was to tackle it head-on. She
could see now that by pretending they were two
different, uninvolved people, they had done more
harm than good. They had been enjoying a superficial
ceasefire, instead of the armistice she had lulled herself
into believing existed.

Once they had really talked and she had convinced
him of her innocence—as she was sure she could now
that he knew her more intimately—their relationship
would have a proper chance to grow. This time it
would be love between two real people, instead of two
actors.

Her decision cheered her so that she was whistling
under her breath when she emerged from the shower,
towelling her hair dry. She decided to confront Traig
right now, before she had a chance to change her
mind.

But as she approached the kitchen door, she slowed, surprised to hear a voice coming from the kitchen. Maybe Oliver Daintree was paying one of his rare visits, although he wasn't the kind of man to linger and chat.

Traig was standing with his back to her when she pushed open the kitchen door. There was no sign of Oliver, or anyone else. Then Traig turned slightly and she caught sight of the telephone cradled in the crook of his shoulder.

'Of course I'll take the damned responsibility,' he was saying in an angry undertone. 'I've told you, you can talk to Drew when I say so and not before. Goodbye.' He slammed the receiver down and only then became aware of Drew standing in the doorway. 'Oh! I didn't hear you come out of the shower.'

She kept her voice steady with an effort. 'Obviously not. Would you mind explaining what that was all about—and don't give me any more lies about it being your business associates.'

'All right. It was Garth Dangerfield. I told him you weren't well enough to talk to him.'

'You told him. . . .' she exploded. 'What gives you the right to speak for me?'

'The right of someone who cares for you. That's what you hired me for, remember? To look after you as a wife would do a husband. I thought I was doing a pretty good job.'

'Better than I suspected, it seems.' Looking at him, the picture of anxiety and contrition, she wished she could believe that concern for her had been his only motive in screening her calls. He must have been doing it since they got here, which explained why she'd had such a peaceful stay. She should have known that something was amiss. Now, she had to know the worst. 'What did Garth want?'

'He's having some problems with the Pacific Centre project.'

A chill of foreboding ran through her. It must be serious for Garth to disturb her when he knew she was here on doctor's orders. 'What sort of problems?' she asked in a strangled tone.

'There's been a strike at the site.'

'A strike? My God, and you didn't think I should be bothered by it! What are you trying to do to me?'

'As I said—protect you. Dangerfield's in charge. He should be able to handle his own labour problems.'

Everything was suddenly, blindingly clear. How could she have missed it for a minute? 'You planned this, didn't you?' she said accusingly.

'Oh, sure. I planned for you to collapse then bribed the doctor to prescribe a holiday. Be sensible, Drew!'

'I think I'm being more sensible than at any time since we got here. Of course I didn't mean to suggest that you planned the circumstances which brought us here. But it didn't take you long to work out how to use them to your advantage, did it?'

He looked at her in amazement. 'What in hell do you mean by that?'

'I mean you already knew I was attracted to you when I thought you were Christopher Traig. So you decided to play on that to distract me so I wouldn't realise how strange it was, not to have any calls from the office.'

His expression turned to one of disgust. 'What could I possibly gain from doing that?'

'Time,' she said painfully. 'Even a fool like Inky Hedges could work it out. We both know if my company runs more than ten per cent over time on the project, Monroe's can move in as consultants, looking like white knights in shining armour at our expense. By screening my calls you made sure I wouldn't know about the trouble at the site in time to do anything about it, increasing your chances of getting into the act. You used me,' she whispered, hurt almost beyond bearing.

'The way you used Garth Dangerfield to steal my plans for you?' he threw at her. 'It takes one to know one, after all.'

She slumped against the kitchen counter, thankful she had something solid to hold on to. 'I've told you over and over—I had nothing to do with stealing your plans. Why won't you believe that.'

'For the same reason you won't believe that I only had your interests at heart by not letting your calls through. We just don't trust each other and probably never will. So if you'll excuse me, *Miss Dominick*, I'll contact Lord Howe Island and see how soon your plane can pick us up.'

Choking with the effort of holding back her tears, she stumbled to the bedroom and began throwing her clothes into a suitcase. So they were back to being Traig and Miss Dominick again. Drew and Christopher, lovers, might never have existed. Except that they *had* existed and the ache in her loins was a reminder of what they had meant to each other. What a fool she was for deluding herself that he loved her. A still bigger fool for expecting him to propose marriage. He hadn't been honest with her since they met so why should she be so surprised if he lied to her now?

She only knew that she was surprised and terribly, terribly hurt. Her first impulse was to banish him from her life as swiftly as possible. She could pay out his absurd contract in cash and there would be nothing he could do about it. Why hadn't she thought of that before? On the other hand, she could keep a closer eye on him when he was working for her.

'Is that the real reason you want to keep him

around?' she asked her dewy-eyed reflection in the mirror. 'Or is it because you can't bear to let him go?'

The Pacific Centre site was a shambles when they arrived there, having driven straight from the airport. The plane had been unable to collect them until the following morning so it was almost a full day after Garth's phone call before she could get to the site.

After threading her way through a line of cat-calling men waving picket signs, she went straight to the site office expecting to find Garth there. She was told he was out inspecting the safety provisions which were the subject of the dispute. At once, she donned the regulation hard hat and went in search of him. She was dimly aware that Traig accompanied her unasked, but she was too intent on resolving the problem at hand to send him away now.

She found Garth among the lower levels of the giant building which was taking shape rapidly. Garth's expression became troubled when he saw her. 'Drew! They told me you were too ill to be involved in this.'

'Never mind that, I'm here now. What's the trouble?'

In theory, the dispute which had halted work was over inadequate safety provisions for the men. But in fact, the real issue was money. The union had somehow found out about the tight deadline for the project and was using it as leverage to gain extra pay for their members, knowing the company was unable to refuse.

'How much do they want?'

Garth paled. 'You can't be thinking of giving in to them?'

'I don't know what else we can do. The real issue isn't safety so increasing to provisions won't solve anything. They'll only find something else to complain about, and we daren't run the risk of rolling strikes.'

'We daren't run over budget either. Paying the crews more won't leave us much profit margin.'

She was uncomfortably aware that Traig was listening intently to all of this. How he must be enjoying her discomfort. The prospect of reducing their already-slim profit margin worried her but if they had to call Monroe's in as consultants, there was a good chance their profit for the year would be wiped out altogether. Was that what Traig wanted? Her father had feared that the rival firm would try to destroy them one day. She would never forgive herself if she was the one who made it possible. Anything was better than that. 'Pay them,' she said shortly.

'But Drew. . . .'

'There is another way,' a commanding voice intervened.

Garth gave Traig a scathing look. 'What's *he* doing here?'

In the drama of their hurried trip to the site, she had forgotten that Garth saw Traig as a rival for her affections. 'He's here because I want him to be,' she said sharply and was aware of a look of surprise from Traig. It was quickly replaced by the impassive mask he had worn since she caught him intercepting her phone calls. 'Don't tell me you want to help us,' she said, not trying to hide her disbelief.

'Is that so surprising!'

'After your behaviour on the island, yes,' she hissed. Garth looked confused, not understanding but aware that there was more going on between them than the surface exchange he was witnessing.

He stepped between them, his expression sulky. 'We're not interested in anything that wonder boy has to suggest,' he said nastily.

Traig ignored him and addressed himself to Drew. 'Do you want to hear my suggestion?'

'I can't wait,' she said dryly, 'although I can't see why you're being so helpful all of a sudden.'

'I have to deal with the same unions that you do. If they can blackmail one employer into paying higher wages, everyone in the industry will suffer.'

She should have known that his motives would be selfish. Hadn't she learned enough in the last few days to know that he would go to any lengths to achieve his own ends? But whatever his motives she couldn't ignore anything which might help solve the present problem. The only thing which mattered right now was the future of Pacific Centre. 'All right, what's your idea?' she asked.

'We reason with the strikers.'

Unaccountably she was disappointed. Was that the best he could suggest? She had been hoping for something more, somehow.

Garth laughed openly. 'Reason with that rabble? You must be joking! Besides, we've already tried talking to them. What do you think I've been doing since the strike started?'

Traig's fists clenched but he held his arms rigidly at his sides. 'I didn't say talk *to* them, I said reason *with* them. Union members are human beings, too. If they are made to understand that co-operation will mean the difference between saving their jobs and their futures, I'm sure they'll listen.'

'I might have known you'd be in favour of talk,' Garth snorted, looking to Drew for support.

'Do you have a better idea?' she asked him pointedly.

The expression of triumph quickly vanished from his face. 'Well, no, I . . . I just know it isn't going to work.'

'We have nothing to lose by trying.' Unconsciously, she squared her shoulders. 'I'll talk to them.'

Traig placed a restraining hand on her arm. 'I didn't mean you. When I suggested reasoning with them, I had myself in mind. You're not fully recovered yet.'

She looked at the hand which rested on her arm but said nothing for a long moment. Then she lifted her eyes and met his gaze squarely. 'Traig Monroe,' she said softly but with deadly emphasis, 'however much you might like it to be so, this is still Dominick Developments and you don't run it yet.'

The impassive mask slid back into place over his features as he slowly and carefully removed his hand.

Her stomach was churning with nerves as Garth led the way across the site to the demountable canteen building where he had asked the men to assemble. She almost wished she had agreed to let Traig handle this for her. But it was her company, not his, and it was her duty to handle the unpleasant tasks as well as the more enjoyable ones. Her father had never shirked an unpleasant task and she didn't intend to either.

The wolf whistles which followed her progress made her wish that, despite the urgency of the problem, she had taken the time to go home and change before coming here. She was dressed in loose silk pants and a cross-over top which thrust her well-formed breasts outwards and accentuated the cleft between them. The outfit was even a little conservative for the island but it was out of place now, when she needed to play down her femininity and make the men respect her as their employer.

A trickle of perspiration escaped from under the tight band of her hard hat. She dashed it away, annoyed that of all the people who might have noticed this sign of her nervousness, the only one who did was Traig.

Her worst fears were confirmed when she walked into the room where the men waited. They were mostly labourers—big, brawny men who hefted slabs of concrete as if they were toys. They cheered and clapped when she entered and she had to close her ears to the worst of the suggestions which greeted her.

'Don't say I didn't warn you,' Traig said in an undertone.

Although she bristled with annoyance at this comment, she was absurdly glad that he was at her side. Somehow she knew he would never allow any physical harm to come to her.

She took a deep breath to steady herself. 'Good day. You all know who I am. . . .'

'Yeah! We kiss your picture in the locker room every morning,' one of the men called.

'She doesn't look anything like the picture,' another heckler added. 'But then she's got all her clothes on now.'

She could feel the colour rushing to her cheeks but willed it away. She wouldn't blush now, she couldn't. But before she could think of a suitable comment which wouldn't provoke a fresh wave of ribald jokes, Traig stepped forward.

'There's something else you should recognise about this lady,' he said calmly. Although he hadn't raised his voice he managed to project it over the noise the group was making. They fell grudgingly silent, waiting for him to elaborate. 'You should all recognise her signature,' he went on. Even Drew was puzzled. What was he talking about? When he knew he had their attention, he concluded, 'on your pay cheques every week.'

Traig's broad hint was not wasted on the men.

Grumbling, they subsided into their seats and waited sullenly for Drew to make her speech.

Appealing to their self-interest had seemed like a good idea when Traig suggested it, but looking at the sea of defiant faces which confronted her, she wondered how much chance her appeal would have. 'They're human beings,' Traig had said. With that in mind, she launched into an eloquent description of the challenge they shared in completing Pacific Centre.

The men shifted restlessly in their seats, plainly bored with what they saw as company rhetoric which had very little to do with their problems. She glanced helplessly at Traig. She was losing them.

He came to his feet in a fluid movement and positioned himself alongside her. 'What Miss Dominick is leading up to is the fact that everyone in this organisation benefits from finishing on schedule and on budget. To that end, the company has decided to offer a cash bonus to every man who helps to pull it off. Isn't that right, Drew?'

Inwardly, she was furious at the high-handed way he had backed her into a corner like this. The men were watching her expectantly. She forced a smile to her lips. 'Of course, I couldn't have put it better myself.'

There was a moment's silence, then a scattering of applause and the first signs of smiles she had seen since she came in. However, one man stood up, his expression still hostile. 'That's all very well, but this dispute was about safety, not money. You're implying we can be bought off.'

Now look what Traig had done with his interference! 'Of course, we're suggesting no such thing,' she assured the man. 'If you'll let me finish, I was about to say that your log of claims will be examined and acted upon right away. Safety is as important to me as it is to you.'

The applause was more enthusiastic this time when she sat down, and she breathed an inward sigh of relief. The men talked among themselves for a few minutes, then the hostile one whom she now recognised as the union delegate, got to his feet and grudgingly agreed to accept the company's proposals and return to work.

When the last of the men had filed out, and Garth had gone with the union leader to thrash out the terms of the bonus, Drew rounded on Traig. 'What did you mean, cutting in on me like that?'

'You can't deny it was the right move to make.'

'I was going to make it, if you'd given me the chance.'

Traig shrugged. 'I would have, but the men wouldn't. They were ready to get up and walk out. You know it as well as I do.'

She *did* know it, but there was no way she was going to admit it to him. He had no right to take over like that. Besides which, there was still something bothering her. 'Why did you bail me out, anyway? You stand to gain more if the project falls behind.'

His eyes flashed his anger and frustration with her. 'You're determined to cast me as the villain, aren't you? You've got such a bee in your bonnet about my company waiting like vultures to take over that you won't even accept a helping hand when it's offered. I've told you before, all I want is simple justice.'

'Admit the plans were stolen from you and all will be forgiven, is that it?'

'Not quite, but it would be a start. *Are* you prepared to admit it?'

'Of course not. You've done enough damage to my peace of mind as it is. I won't have you accusing Garth Dangerfield unjustly.'

'What if it wasn't unjust?' he asked softly.

'I've only your word for that and it isn't enough.'
She pushed her hair back from her face in a weary
gesture. 'Since you're still my employee, I'm within
my rights to forbid you to mention your charges to
Garth.'

'That doesn't stop you from mentioning them,' he
said, seeming unperturbed by her reminder of their
relative status. Damn him! Why didn't he defy her,
resign—anything but accept her domination over him
with this infuriating unconcern?

'Why should I?' she demanded.

'Because you're a woman of honour. I admire your
loyalty to Garth but deep down, you want to know the
truth and you won't be happy until you do.'

She cursed him for reading her so well, a legacy
of the long nights they had spent talking together on
the verandah at Honeymoon Island. With a start,
she realised that he now knew her better than any
man alive—both mentally and physically. She felt
herself colouring at the memory, and she pressed
both palms to her face to cool her burning cheeks.
Despite her reminder that he was still her employee,
they both knew that they were rivals again. The
rapport they had shared on the island was gone,
banished by mutual suspicion and mistrust. She
sighed deeply.

At once, he was attentive. 'Are you feeling ill
again?'

He was acting his part superbly, she thought wryly.
'No, I'm fine,' she assured him, not wanting to
encourage him to take his pretence of concern any
further. 'This has been rather tiring, that's all. I think
I'll go home for a while.'

'But you *will* tackle Garth about the origin of the
plans?' he insisted.

'I don't know,' she demurred. But inside, she knew

that she must, for her own peace of mind. The only problem was, how to ask Garth without making him feel as if resigning was the only way to defend himself. Pacific Centre needed him, *she* needed him—but she also needed to know the truth.

CHAPTER SIX

HER chance to arrange a talk with Garth came when he called at her office to report on progress at the site. It seemed that, for once, everything was going according to schedule.

'The bonus did the trick then?' she said happily.

Garth's smile faded. 'I've been meaning to talk to you about that. I'm sure we could have got the men back to work without the extra cost. That meddling Monroe only made the suggestion so it would cost you money.'

'If he hadn't suggested paying the men a bonus, I was going to,' she said, noting Garth's annoyed reaction. 'Dad always said people work harder at something if they have a personal stake in it.'

'I suppose that's true,' he agreed with obvious reluctance. 'But I wouldn't like to think you were being influenced by that character.'

Remembering that Traig had been instrumental in getting Garth fired from his job at Monroe's, Drew could understand his feelings. She decided to change the subject. 'Have we been able to get those structural steel sections at the price originally quoted by the suppliers?'

Garth's smile widened. 'We've done better than that. The stuff is already on site. I found a supplier who actually undercut the original quote.'

This was surprising news indeed. 'But how could they do that? They would have had to absorb two price rises since those quotes were issued.'

Garth spread his hands wide in a gesture of appeal.

'Trust me,' he said, then drew his brows together. 'I hope you still do—if Monroe hasn't managed to undermine your faith in me, too.'

Not for want of trying, she thought wryly. Aloud, she said brightly, 'Of course not. I make my own judgments about the people who work for me.'

He leaned across her desk, his eyes imploring. 'In that case, have dinner with me tomorrow night.'

She hesitated. 'I don't know, Garth. Things are very difficult at the moment.'

His lip curled into a sneer and he straightened. 'I knew it. Monroe *is* getting to you.'

Was he getting to her, as Garth put it? Yes, but not in the way Garth suspected. She wondered what he would say if he knew how she and Traig had spent their time together on the island. Garth was still under the impression that she had gone there alone. He would be furious if he knew that Traig had been with her. Now she knew how a bone felt when it was being tugged back and forth between two dogs. 'All right, Garth,' she said heavily, 'I'll have dinner with you.' It would placate him and give her the chance she needed to ask him about the plans.

He brightened at once. 'That's more like it. I'll pick you up at your place at seven.'

By seven o'clock the next evening, she was still in two minds about the wisdom of going out with him. He thought she had agreed because she returned his feelings. In reality, she saw it as an ideal opportunity to probe the truth or otherwise of Traig's allegations. Over dinner Garth was less likely to become offended by her questioning. If his plans for Pacific Centre *were* original, conceived after Garth joined Dominick Developments, then no one would be hurt and her mind would be at rest. That she would also be forced to admit that Garth was right and Traig was out to make mischief, she found strangely disquieting. If only the question could be settled without hurting either Garth or Traig—or herself! 'You can't make an omelette without breaking eggs,' she recalled someone once telling her. Yet somehow, she had to find a way.

Punctually at seven, she heard Garth's car pull up. Bosun raced to the front door, barking frantically to let her know that someone was outside.

She reached down to ruffle his ears. 'It's okay, boy. It's a friend.'

He refused to be mollified and kept up a low, throaty growl from the moment Garth came into the living room. 'That dog doesn't like me,' he observed.

'He's just trying to prove what a brave watchdog he is,' she assured him, but wondered why the little animal never acted this way with Traig.

Garth looked around uneasily. 'Where's wonder boy?'

'He's out for the evening, and I wish you wouldn't call him that.'

'Sorry,' he apologised unconvincingly. 'I forgot for a moment who my boss is.'

'I didn't mean anything like that and you know it,' she said crossly. 'Let's not argue tonight.'

'Of course not,' he agreed, softening at once. 'Tonight it will be just Garth and Drew.'

Garth and Drew. On the island it had been Christopher and Drew, with Traig and Miss Dominick pushed firmly into the background. As they made their way out to Garth's maroon Bluebird, she wondered why men found it so hard to cope with all of her—the woman and the company director. She had no trouble reconciling both halves of her character yet they seemed to find it a problem. As long as she was pretty, feminine Drew they knew how to treat her, but as soon as she assumed her mantle of profesionalism, they pulled back as if she could bite. She sighed. Women still had a long way to go before their equality was accepted as more than just a word.

'Why the big sigh?' Garth queried holding the car door open for her.

His gesture only emphasised what she had been thinking. 'Nothing important,' she said aloud, determined not to say anything to spoil the tone of the evening.

He took her to a lovely old restaurant which had once been a Cobb & Co staging house. It had massively thick stone walls and open fireplaces, with the gleam of highly polished timber everywhere. The original small rooms had been knocked into one larger one, the dividing walls being shaped into arches to create intimate areas furnished with only two or three tables in each one. Imitation oil lamps hung from the ceiling and artefacts from the days of convict settlement decorated the walls.

'This is charming,' she enthused when they were seated at their table and the waiter had handed them their menus. 'However did you find it?' Since it was located on a side road some way out of Sydney, she had not even known it was here.

'Oh, it's the in place at the moment,' Garth told her. 'It used to be very quiet and exclusive, then Dolores Hartman wrote about it in her column and everybody who was anybody flocked here.'

At the mention of the columnist's name, Drew remembered she was supposed to have given her an exclusive story about her so-called romance with Traig Monroe. She had concocted the lie to deter Inky Hedges at her party, then had forgotten about it when she went off to the island. She hoped Hedges had also forgotten about it by now.

'I'm having the Bushman's Banquet,' Garth said, breaking into her thoughts.

She looked at the listing on the menu. It was a clever name for barbecued steak with all the trimmings, and sounded rather substantial. 'I'll have the rabbit in champagne,' she decided instead. 'It sounds delicious.'

'It is, I've had it myself. They cook the rabbit fillets in a champagne sauce with green grapes.'

'Oh no,' she breathed.

'Don't you like green grapes?'

'No, it isn't that. Look who's zeroing in on us.'

Her hope that Inky Hedges had forgotten about her was dashed when he came sashaying up to their table. 'Hello children,' he gushed, then completely ignored Garth to address himself to Drew. 'I've been following la Hartman's column ever since your party but she hasn't written a word about you and Monroe.'

'That's because there's nothing to write.'

'Yet,' he corrected. He looked at Garth, seeming to see him for the first time. 'I must say I'm surprised to see you here with someone else.'

Garth coloured hotly and opened his mouth as if to make an angry retort but Drew put a hand on his arm. 'It's all right, Garth. Some people's opinions are not worth commenting on.' To Inky, she said coldly, 'I can't see what's so surprising about me having dinner with a business associate.'

'Neither can I,' Hedges agreed mildly, 'unless one's live-in boyfriend is also here, with another woman.'

She followed the direction of his gaze to where Traig was seated in another alcove, his dark sculptured head bent close to that of a young woman. They must have come in after Drew and Garth, because that table had been empty when they passed it.

From where she sat, Drew could see that the girl possessed flawless skin tanned honey gold, and startlingly pretty golden hair which she wore in a curling cap, framing a heart-shaped face. She was talking animatedly to Traig and he was smiling back in a way which tore at Drew's heartstrings.

Why the sight should bother her, she wasn't quite sure but it shook her to the core. It took all her self-possession she had learned since taking over the company not to let Hedges see the effect his bombshell had on her.

In all the time she had known him as Christopher and then as Traig, she had never stopped to think that there might be a woman in his life. Carrying out his duties as her employee—which he still insisted on doing—and overseeing his own company kept him fully occupied so he had done almost no socialising that she knew of, since he came to work for her. Nevertheless, he was a man with normal male needs, and since she had spurned him after that fateful night on the island, she should have expected him to look elsewhere to satisfy his desires.

Hedges was watching her intently. 'I had a feeling you didn't know,' he observed quietly, 'I'm sorry.'

She looked up at him in astonishment. 'You're what?'

'Don't look so surprised, darling. I do have feelings even if my job won't let me indulge them.'

'Does that mean you won't be writing about this?'

He waved a hand airily. 'Maybe, and maybe not. We'll see. I have a feeling there's a bigger story here than you and Monroe are letting on, and I intend to keep digging till I find it. Bye-bye, dears, enjoy your dinner.'

'What a strange man he is,' Drew commented after the columnist had left. 'That's the first time he's ever let on that he minds having to tear people's reputations to shreds for a living.'

'You haven't helped by giving him so much ammunition,' Garth said grumpily. 'Of all the people you could hire to run your house, why does it have to be Monroe? Doesn't he have enough to do running his own show?'

She was saved from having to answer by the arrival of the waiter with their dinner. While he decanted and poured the wine and Garth went through the ritual of sampling it, Drew's gaze travelled irresistibly to the table at the far corner of the room.

As she watched, Traig reached across and rested a hand on the girl's arm and a shudder of longing went through Drew. Then he looked up and his eyes met Drew's. A sensation like electricity passed through her body. As if by a signal, they both turned their attention quickly to their own dinner partners. It was tit-for-tat, and yet Drew sensed that Traig was as disturbed at seeing her here with Garth as she was to see him with another woman.

Then a waiter brought a telephone to Traig's table and hovered while he took the call. Whatever it was, it brought a wide smile to his lips and he jumped up, pulling the girl's chair out for her with boyish eagerness. Without looking back at Drew, he tossed money on to the table and went out with his arm around the girl's shoulders. A feverish sensation tore along Drew's veins. Unwillingly, she recognised the feeling as jealousy!

Garth looked to where she was staring and smiled in satisfaction. 'Good, they've gone. I couldn't relax while he was here, knowing he was spying on us.'

'What makes you think that?' she asked in surprise.

'I know him.' He grabbed her hand and leaned closer. 'Look, I know you must have good reason for having him in your house but you must get rid of him. He's spying on us, I'm positive.'

She tried to make light of his plea. 'In that case, surely it's better to have him where we can see him? That way, we know what he's up to.'

Garth pouted in annoyance. 'I think Inky Hedges is right. You've fallen in love with Monroe.'

'My feelings have nothing to do with our working relationship, Garth.'

He snorted in disgust. 'Working relationship! We had more than a working relationship before *he* came along.'

'That's not true, Garth. We went out a few times, but I never let you think there was anything more to it.'

His expression grew pleading. 'Please don't let's argue. We were having a lovely time until Monroe turned up.'

She couldn't argue the truth of that. Making a conscious effort to relax, she picked at the rabbit dish she had ordered. It was delicious, but seeing Traig with the other woman had destroyed her appetite. Nevertheless, she did her best to do justice to the dish to avoid further questioning from Garth.

She declined the offer of a dessert, and settled for black coffee and after-dinner mints. Belatedly, she remembered why she had come here in the first place. They had reached their second bottle of wine by now and Garth's mood was much more mellow so now was the best time to broach the subject of the stolen plans.

'I think your ideas for Pacific Centre were outstanding,' she began and he glowed with pleasure. 'When did you first get the idea for the design?'

He looked down at the tablecloth and began to arrange the cutlery into patterns. 'I can't remember,' he muttered, not looking at her.

'But it was such an inspired move to combine residential units with the commercial space,' she persisted. 'Personally, I would have been scared off by the zoning laws—but you even saw a way to satisfy both the award judges and the city council. I'd love to know how you worked it all out.'

'Why the third degree about where I got the idea?' Garth growled suddenly. 'I suppose Monroe's been saying I stole it from him?'

Now why would Garth say such a thing? She had given him no clues to the reason for her interest. Unless . . . a chill ran down her spine as she seriously considered that the plans might have been stolen after all. She was tempted to ask Garth outright but she didn't want to do that until she had more to go on. 'Traig did seem to think his award entry had a lot of similarity to ours,' she dissembled.

'Just like him!' Garth exploded. 'He won't be happy until he finds some evidence to support his stupid charges, then I'll be eased out the way I was at Monroe's. He's got it in for me, I tell you.'

Tiredly, she massaged her brow with one hand. 'You're being unreasonable. He can't find any proof if none exists, can he?'

'All I know is he managed to turn Darcy Monroe against me, after I'd been more like a son to him than his real son who was too busy gallivanting around overseas.'

This conversation was getting them nowhere. She wasn't going to resolve her suspicions tonight. If anything, Garth's evasiveness had only added to them. She was also disturbed by the fanatical gleam which came into his eyes when he talked about Traig. His resentment of Traig was obviously deep-rooted and could be destructive. She would have to avoid fuelling it if she could.

She stood up and collected her things. 'I'd like to go home now, if you don't mind. I'm very tired.'

'Of course. I'd forgotten about your illness. I shouldn't have kept you out so late.'

He was consideration itself on the drive home, tucking a travel rug around her legs like a mother hen, although the car heater was more than adequate. 'I had exhaustion, not frostbite,' she laughed.

'I just don't want anything to happen to you while you're in my care.'

It was only when they reached her front door that his attitude changed. His arms went around her and he pulled her hard against him. She tried to struggle free but he held her fast. 'Don't fight it,' he said hoarsely. 'I've dreamed of kissing you and I know you feel the same way.'

'Please, Garth, don't. I like you, but it isn't enough.'

She was afraid he was going to kiss her against her will but her last comment seemed to bring him to his senses. 'You like me,' he said scathingly, releasing her. 'Is that the best you can do? It's Monroe, isn't it? I'll bet you have more than liking for him.'

'Stop it,' she said sharply. 'I don't think we'd better go out again, Garth, for both our sakes. Goodnight.'

Quickly, she dodged inside and shut her door, leaning against it gratefully. Through the timber she heard Garth stride off down the path, then his car engine roared into life and he drove off with a squeal of tyres.

It had been a mistake agreeing to go out with him tonight. She was no nearer to finding out the truth about the Pacific Centre plans and had only succeeded in creating friction between herself and Garth.

Damn! Why did Traig Monroe have to come here with his ugly suspicions in the first place? She had only his word that the plans were stolen and he admitted that he had no way of proving it. Perhaps Garth was right and he was only out to sow discord at Dominick's.

Somehow, she couldn't accept that. On the island, she had come to know Traig intimately and she was sure he would never stoop to such tactics. For whatever reason, he believed he was in the right, otherwise he wouldn't be pursuing the matter.

She had told Garth she was tired and she had been at the restaurant, but now she was too restless to go to bed. She showered and changed into a velvet housegown, then curled up on the couch in the living room, delighting Bosun who was only too glad to keep her company.

'You don't know how lucky you are, being a dog,' she told him as she fondled his flop-ears. 'No problems about love or hate, no suspicion, no jealousy.' She stumbled a little over the last word, knowing it applied to herself. There was no other way to describe the searing sensation she had experienced at the sight of Traig and his companion.

'If only I'd never started this stupid "wife" business,' she said to Bosun, who wagged his tail uncertainly. 'It's all right, boy, I know you don't understand.' It had seemed like a lark at first, having a man to do for her all the things a woman traditionally did for a husband. 'But for one thing,' Traig had corrected her. In the end, he had even fulfilled that role—so well in fact, that her body throbbed at the memory. But there was more to a marriage than having someone to take care of the housekeeping and cooking or provide a shoulder to cry on. To be truly husband and wife—whoever filled each role—there had to be a deeper commitment, and that's what was missing. Even though he had taken her to his bed, Traig was a spouse in name only. There was no commitment, nor was there ever likely to be.

She choked on a sob, realising now that she yearned for such a commitment. If only Maggie had never suggested the idea in the first place! But she could hardly blame her assistant. Drew herself had been the one who followed it through. Well, she was paying for her folly now.

The scratch of a key in the front door told her Traig had arrived home. She was surprised to see from the clock how long she had sat there lost in thought. Bosun jumped up and ran to greet Traig, his feathery tail threshing furiously.

'You rate a much better greeting than Garth,' she said when Traig came into the living room.

'But only from Bosun, it seems. I didn't expect to find you still awake. Dangerfield must be better company than I thought if he could hold your interest till this hour.'

She felt a sudden urge to hurt him as much as he had hurt her with his duplicity. 'That's pretty rich, coming from you,' she retorted. 'Your blonde friend seems to have been equally stimulating to keep you out this late.'

'You think she was my girlfriend,' he asked, his voice cold.

'What else? You certainly didn't waste any more time than you had to over the meal. Where did you go in such a hurry—her apartment?'

He looked at her in disgust. 'Is that what you think? What a mind you must have! As a matter of fact, I've been at the hospital. My father has regained considerably more movement. It's been happening slowly for the last few days. Then tonight at the restaurant, I got a call to say he was lucid and asking for me.'

Her hand flew to her mouth. 'Oh Traig, I'm so sorry! I didn't mean all the things I said. I was just. . . .'

'Jealous?' he supplied.

She looked away before he could see that his shot had gone home. 'I'm so pleased to hear that your father's getting better,' she said, genuine pleasure in her voice.

'Not getting better, but improving,' he amended. 'There's still not much hope, but at least he can communicate now, even if it is with an effort. He's been trying for days, it seems, but his body had only just begun to co-operate.'

'How terrible for him,' she breathed, her eyes wide with sympathy. 'It must have been horrifying for him, imprisoned in his body like that.'

A shudder shook him. 'It was bad enough to make him drive himself to superhuman limits, to regain his power of speech.'

'I wonder what he wanted to communicate that was so important to him,' she mused.

Traig gave her a searching look. 'I was hoping you could tell me that.'

She started in surprise. 'Me? Why?'

'Because it's you he's asking for. He forgot at first that your father was dead. When I reminded him, he said he would have to talk to you instead. It seemed hellishly important to him.'

Whatever could Darcy Monroe want to say to her? She had never met him face to face. He had always been portrayed as an ogre so that, as a child, she had believed that a Monroe was some sort of monster. As she grew older, she gradually realised that they were human beings just like herself, but there any similarity ended.

She had convinced herself that, for her sake, her father would have accepted her relationship with Traig, but Darcy was another matter. It had been Darcy who engineered the deal which almost cost the

Dominicks everything they had. Andrew had trusted Darcy and been betrayed, and had never forgiven him for it. Now she felt as if she would be betraying her father's memory if she agreed to see the old man.

Traig watched the interplay of emotions on her face. 'I know how your father felt about mine,' he said, 'but you can't let that prevent you from granting the wish of a dying man.'

Her head came up at once. 'Dying?'

His anguish was thinly veiled. 'I'm afraid so. His present improvement is a miracle, as much due to his iron will as medical science. But he could have another stroke at any time. The doctors say it will be massive, and final.'

She looked at him wildly, like a trapped animal, 'Traig, I'm so sorry about all this.'

'Sorry won't help,' he said harshly. 'He wants to see you. Will you come?'

'Yes, yes, I'll come—does that satisfy you?' she yelled at him, at the same time sending up a fervent prayer to her father, wherever he was, that he would understand there was nothing else she could do.

She had seen newspaper pictures of Darcy Monroe. He was a wiry man with thick, waving iron-grey hair and piercing eyes. Taller than most men, he tended to stoop as if he had never quite adjusted to his height. The press had been as unkind to him as they were to Drew, in line with an apparent desire to bring down anyone seen as a 'tall poppy'. Andrew Dominick and Darcy Monroe had been two of the tallest poppies in the country and both had been contemptuous of their treatment by the media.

So Drew was shocked when she was confronted by the wasted form of Darcy as he was now. He was so thin that he was almost skeletal, and his hair had turned snow white. The only thing she recognised about him as he lay in the tangle of supporting machinery, was the glint in the grey eyes. If there was any doubt as to whether Darcy's brain still functioned to the full, one look at those eyes dispelled it. He knew exactly what was going on, and his frustration with his present limitations was evident in the look he gave to Traig when he walked in followed by Drew.

'I've brought her as requested, Dad,' Traig said with forced good humour.

Darcy's right hand clenched convulsively on the bedclothes, but Drew noticed that his left hand didn't move at all. 'G-g-good,' he said with an obvious effort.

Her emotions were stirred by the plight of the once-mighty tycoon, but her heart ached most for Traig. What this must be doing to him! She could only compare it with how she would have felt if it had been Andrew lying here like this. She knew she couldn't have borne it.

Yet Traig was laughing and joking to his father about everyday events, as if nothing was wrong, although Darcy could only answer in monosyllables. Her admiration of Traig increased until she felt as if her heart would burst with it.

The old man reached out a trembling hand towards Drew. 'Dom ... dom ... Miss Dominick,' he said at last, getting the words out clearly.

She fixed a smile on her face and went to him, taking the withered hand. 'Hello, Mr Monroe. I've heard a lot about you.'

The skin around his eyes crinkled and she could sense that he was laughing inwardly. 'I know you can imagine what I must have heard,' she went on, warming to the old man so that awareness of his condition receded. 'I grew up thinking that a Monroe had two heads. I'm relieved to find you only have one.'

Darcy was shaking with amusement now. 'Dom-Dominicks, too,' he said.

'You thought we had two heads?' she supplied. When he nodded, she smiled. 'Then maybe it's just as well we've finally met to put an end to such rumours.'

Darcy turned his head towards Traig who sat on the edge of the bed. 'Like her,' he chuckled.

'Seems you've won yourself a heart,' Traig said. 'Who'd have believed it?'

Not her father, she thought ruefully. It was tragic that they had to meet like this—only able to bury the hatchet when death loomed over one of them. It was such a waste! 'You had something you wanted to tell me, Mr Monroe,' she prompted gently.

He arched his eyebrows in a clear expression of puzzlement. 'Tell? What?' he asked.

Traig moved around to the right side of the bed to place himself on what she now recognised as Darcy's 'good side'. His other side appeared to be useless. 'Dad, you asked me to bring Drew here because you had something important to tell her.'

There was a brief flaring of memory in the grey eyes then he closed them. 'Can't . . . remember . . . was . . . something,' he forced out.

To Drew's horror she saw a tear force its way out from under the old man's closed eyelid. She squeezed his hand hard. 'It's all right, Mr Monroe. You'll remember what it was, I'm sure. Just give yourself time.'

Even as she said it, she knew that time was one thing Darcy Monroe didn't have. Still, she couldn't stand by and watch him distress himself like this. She would have to be patient and hope he remembered what he had wanted to tell her.

Suddenly, Darcy opened his eyes again and his grip on her hand tightened. She was surprised by the

strength in his hold. His willpower was amazing! 'No
. . . must tell. . . .' he said urgently, his eyes wide with
the effort of getting the words out.

They became alarmed as he tried to sit up in the bed
and Drew reached for the button which would
summon the nurse. As soon as she saw the state her
patient was in, the nurse chased them all from the
room and called in Darcy's doctor.

Outside in the corridor, Drew leaned against the
cool white wall and closed her eyes.

'I'm sorry I had to put you through that for
nothing,' Traig said beside her. 'He was so insistent
the last time.'

'Don't be sorry,' she said without opening her eyes.
She didn't want him to see that they were wet with
tears of admiration for the old man's wonderful spirit.
'I'm glad I had the chance to meet him.'

'I'm glad, too. He's heard so much about you that
he was keen to meet you.'

This time she did open her eyes wide with surprise.
'Heard about me? From whom?'

He scuffed the toe of one shoe against the other and
gave the act his whole attention. 'From me. You see,
all the time he was unable to talk, I sat with him and
talked to him. I told him everything.'

'Everything?' she said in a whisper.

He smiled at last and she had a heart-stirring
glimpse of the man she had known—and loved—on
the island. 'Well, maybe not everything,' he admitted.
'But all about how you decided to hire a man as your
"wife"—and how I conned you into hiring me.'

'But not about the plans?' she said, sure of his
answer before he gave it.

'No, not that. That's between you, me and Garth
Dangerfield. I didn't want to worry Dad. Besides
which, I wasn't even sure he could hear me. It was

only when he could talk again that he told me my ramblings had helped to restore his will to live.'

He slammed his closed fist hard against the brick wall. 'It makes everything else seem so petty, doesn't it?'

She had been thinking the same thing. On impulse, she said, 'It makes me realise life is too precious to waste. Oh, Traig, can't we start again, forget about who's right and who's wrong and just make the most of whatever this thing is between us? You said yourself you have no proof that Garth stole your plans.'

His jaw tilted determinedly and the implacable look came back into his eyes. 'I wish I could, Drew, but it isn't that simple. If I give in now, every time I pass that building the knowledge will fester inside me until it destroys everything good between us. What I've started, I must finish. Can't you understand that?'

'No, I can't. All I know is you're determined to destroy both of us with your obsession.' She started to walk away but he caught at her arm.

'Will you come again?'

There was still the mystery of what Darcy had wanted to tell her so much he risked bringing on a second, fatal stroke to do it. 'I don't know. I'll try,' she said.

CHAPTER SEVEN

As it turned out, she was unable to visit Darcy as often as she would have liked. Work had piled up while she was recovering on the island so it was usually late into the evening before she could even think of getting away.

Darcy was still unable to remember what he had been so anxious to tell her. There were times when his mind wandered and he was unable to recognise either her or Traig. Drew was naturally curious to know what was worrying the old man but decided not to press the point, since he became distressed whenever it was brought up. It might have been important to him but it was unlikely to be very vital to her, she decided.

More than likely it had something to do with the old feud between Darcy and her father. Not so long ago it would have been important to her, too, especially if it helped to bury the hatchet between the two families. As it was, she and Traig seemed to have started to do that for themselves so anything Darcy wanted to add probably wouldn't make much difference.

She had told Traig to take all the time he wished to spend with his father, so he was seldom at home when she arrived, although there was always a hot meal waiting for her to return to.

The contract between them was almost at an end and she would have willingly released him from it, but he stubbornly insisted on honouring it to the letter.

'But why?' she asked. Couldn't he see how his continued presence was affecting her? At night she tossed and turned in bed, tormented by the knowledge that he was asleep only a few doors away. Several

times, she had started to go to him then forced herself
to lie back, reminding herself that until there was
trust between them, there could be no love.

As before, his answer had been that he believed in
finishing what he started.

'You're a stubborn, infuriating man!' she had yelled
at him. At the same time, she knew she wouldn't have
wanted him to be any other way.

Maggie Symmonds came in and dropped some
papers on her desk. 'For you to sign,' she said then
hovered as if debating whether to say something more.

'Yes?' Drew queried.

'You aren't getting much sleep these days, are you?'
Maggie asked.

'Don't mother me, Maggie, please.' While she still
appreciated Maggie's concern, she wished she could
make her understand that something had happened to
her on the island. Now she felt completely grown-up
and able to make personal decisions about her life with
the same assurance with which she'd always made
business ones.

Maggie seemed to sense the change. 'I see,' she said
quietly and gathered up the papers Drew had just
signed.

She immediately regretted her churlish behaviour.
'Don't be offended, Maggie. I just meant. . . .'

'I'm not,' the older woman told her. 'I've been the
nearest thing to a mother to you for most of your life
so I know you pretty well. You went to the island a
girl and you've come back a woman. What worries me
is that it hasn't made you any happier.'

Drew got up and wandered over to the window,
looking out but hardly seeing the view of Sydney's
business district which usually gave her so much
pleasure. 'It has in some ways,' she confessed. 'If only
there weren't so many problems!'

'Problems can be resolved—even if his name *is* Monroe.'

Drew spun around, her eyes widening. 'You know, and you don't mind?'

Maggie shrugged. 'Why should I mind? The old feud was between your father and his so I don't see what it has to do with you two. If you're in love with him, marry him. You can solve any other problems together.'

At once Drew flew across the room and enveloped her assistant in a hug which left her breathless. 'Maggie, you're marvellous,' she breathed.

'Even though I mother you,' the older woman said dryly.

Drew grinned ruefully. 'Even then.'

As soon as Maggie had gone back to her own office, Drew reached for the telephone but hesitated with her hand on the receiver. She had no doubt that Maggie was right. Whatever problems stood between her and Traig could be resolved once they were united by the force of their love for each other. Hadn't she learned enough at his father's bedside to know what really mattered in life? Her only worry was whether Traig would feel the same.

She jumped as the telephone shrilled under her hand. Could it be Traig, calling to tell her he had arrived at the same conclusion? Eagerly, she picked up the receiver. 'Drew Dominick.'

Her spirits dropped when a strange voice came on to the line. 'Miss Dominick? I'm glad I got straight through to you.'

'Who is this, please?'

'Kurt Wilder. I'm one of the consulting engineers on Pacific Centre. We have a problem at the site, a big one.'

'Whatever it is, shouldn't you talk to Garth Dangerfield? He *is* the project co-ordinator.'

'He's also the problem,' Wilder explained.

A cold sensation travelled through her and she gripped the phone more tightly. 'Go ahead,' she said, striving to keep her voice steady.

There was a momentary hesitation, then he said, 'I'd prefer not to discuss it on the phone. Can you come over to the site right away?'

'This had better be important.'

'It is, believe me, Miss Dominick. I wouldn't be troubling you otherwise.'

Slowly, she replaced the receiver, her mind whirling. What could be wrong now? Whatever it was, the engineer believed that Garth was involved so that ruled out anything as simple as more labour problems. But what else could it be?

She had thought she was recovered from her exhaustion but she soon discovered differently. The phone call with its disturbing implications had left her shaking from head to foot.

Taking a few deep breaths to steady herself, she called Maggie on the intercom and asked to have a car and driver waiting outside in five minutes. That done, she stared at the phone. There was still time to call Traig and tell him she loved him enough to want to work out their problems.

It would be so easy to make the call. So why didn't she? She wasn't sure why, but she had a feeling that the problem at the site would have a bearing on her relationship with Traig. She left without making the call.

The construction site was only a short drive away from her office but an accident in busy Sussex Street delayed her, fraying her nerves even more by the time she checked in at the site office.

Although his name hadn't meant much to her on the phone, she recognised Kurt Wilder on sight as one of the company's longest serving employees. He was a rugged looking man with sun-weathered features and iron-grey hair. He was alone in the office and stood up when she came in.

'Good afternoon, Kurt. I'm sorry I didn't recognise you over the phone.'

'No reason you should since I was before your time,' he said affably. 'I helped your father start this company and gave it my all for thirty years, but these days I keep what I think they call a low profile.'

Now she remembered. He was officially retired but still enjoyed handling special assignments on occasion. She glanced around the office. 'Is Garth joining us?'

'No, ma'am. That was one reason I wanted you to come over right away. I wanted the chance to talk to you alone, then it will be up to you what you decide to do about it.'

'About what?' she asked, thoroughly baffled. She was also seriously alarmed. Kurt Wilding had been one of the most skilled and conscientious engineers in the industry as well as being devoted to the company's interests. Any problem he uncovered was likely to be disastrous.

It was.

On the desk in front of him lay two samples of steel roofing material. He pushed them towards her. 'How well do you know your building products?'

'I know some of the theory but I'm no expert,' she said.

'Can you tell the difference between these two samples?'

She looked closely at them. 'They look the same to me.'

He nodded. 'They would to most people. I didn't spot the difference myself until I took them over to the Research and Development lab. The sample on the left failed to meet the test requirements for the Australian Standard.'

She had a horrid feeling she knew what was coming next. 'That's the material we're using on the project?'

'I'm afraid so.'

'But how could that happen—how did you spot it?'

'I'll answer your last question first. We fixed most of the sheets last week before we had those heavy winds.'

She had been away at the island at that time but had heard about the freak winds after she returned home. She nodded. 'Go on.'

'The material stood up to the wind-loads but they buckled when we put a maintenance team up there to check that none of the sheets had worked loose.'

Gradually the picture was becoming clear. Roofing sheets which met the required building standards should have been strong enough to cope with men working on them. 'I see,' she said slowly, 'and you think Garth has something to do with this?'

'I'm sure of it. He was the one who cancelled our original order and brought in this stuff from an importer.'

At once Drew remembered how pleased Garth had been that he had obtained the steel at less than quoted prices. She had wondered at the time how they were able to do it. Now she knew. Competition in the building industry was so intense that some suppliers were reducing quality so they could offer cheaper prices than their competitors. The difference in quality might be fractional, but in a job as large as Pacific Centre, the difference in cost could be substantial.

Of course, the fact that Garth had ordered the steel didn't prove that he knew it was below standard. 'Did it agree with the original specifications?' she asked. If it did, Garth was in the clear.

Kurt shook his head. 'I wish I could say it did but it's marginally under what we specified—enough to meet the standard on paper, but not in actual use.'

'I don't understand. How can that be possible?' she asked.

'Well, when the sheeting is manufactured, the way the mill works means the sheets are marginally thinner at the edges than in the middle. If the middle is already the minimum thickness, then the edges will be thinner than specified. The weakness will only show up in a test lab or when somebody gets killed walking on the stuff when it gives way.

Her spirits had been sinking steadily since he began. 'How much of the material is affected?' she asked in a low tone.

'All of it.'

She could hardly believe her ears. This could mean the end of any chance they had of finishing Pacific Centre on time and on budget. 'What on earth did Garth think he was doing?' she asked unhappily.

Kurt shrugged. 'I don't know. I think you'd better ask him that.'

Which was exactly what she intended to do. She left instructions for Garth to report to her no matter how late he returned. She would wait for him at her office.

Maggie clucked disapprovingly when Drew asked her to send out for take-away food. 'You should go out and have a proper meal,' she urged.

'I want to be here when Garth arrives. I have something very important to discuss with him.'

Muttering about Drew being just like her father, Maggie sent for the take-away meal then went home herself.

Left alone in the office, Drew picked at the chicken

dish in the container then pushed it aside. For the first time she wondered if she had bitten off more than she could chew with Pacific Centre. She had seen it as her crowning achievement, the first really big project the company had undertaken under her management. But it had been dogged by misfortune at every step of the way.

First Traig had accused her of stealing his plans for the Centre. Then he had tried to prevent her finding out about the strike—for her own good, he said. She had believed him when he said he didn't care about having a share in the project, but now . . . she wished she could be sure. She still had a nagging feeling he would turn out to be involved in this latest problem.

Her intercom buzzed and she flicked the button. 'Yes?'

'Mr Dangerfield's in the lobby to see you, Miss Dominick.'

She recognised the voice of the security guard at the main entrance. 'Thanks, Geoff, send him up.'

Moments later Garth burst into her office, his agitation plain. 'What's up, Drew? They told me at the site you wanted to see me even if it was midnight.'

'Sit down please, Garth. I have something to discuss with you.'

He took the chair opposite her desk but sat poised on the edge of it while she sketched in the details of the substandard steel she had learned from Kurt Wilding this afternoon.

As she reached the end of her tale, he burst out, 'You can't think I would deliberately order poor quality steel?'

She looked down at her hands. 'I don't know what to think, Garth. I wanted to hear your side of things before I made up my mind.'

From chalk white, his skin turned mottled with annoyance. 'My side? Then you *do* think I'm guilty!'

'I didn't say that.'

'You may as well have. Well I'm not going to dignify this business by explaining myself to anyone, including you. I did what I thought was best. . . .'

'For you or the project?' she asked quietly.

He jumped to his feet and rested both hands on her desk so he was looming over her, his eyes wild. 'It's Monroe, isn't it? He's accused me. . . .'

'The lab tests accused you,' she said, putting all the authority she could muster into her voice. 'The steel that was delivered simply didn't measure up under lab testing. People's lives are at stake here—didn't you realise that?'

'It seems like you already have me tried and convicted in your mind,' he said sullenly, but slumped back into his chair and crossed his arms defensively over his chest.

'It isn't like that at all. I asked you to explain your side of this. Since you refuse. . . .'

'If I refused, it was for your sake,' he said unexpectedly, the fanatical gleam returning to his eyes.

She looked at him in bewilderment. 'For my sake? I don't understand.'

'I was hoping to spare you. I know how you feel about Traig Monroe, even though he isn't worthy to clean your boots.'

'Wait a minute. What does Traig have to do with this?'

'Everything. He was the one who put me up to the whole thing. He gave me the address of the importer and the letters of introduction. But he assured me the stuff was up to specifications, otherwise I wouldn't have touched it, I swear.'

The premonition of disaster she'd been having ever since Kurt's phone call returned and she shivered, although the office was warm. 'I think you'd better start from the beginning.'

'Monroe knew about the consultant's clause before we did,' Garth began. 'He's been planning to muscle in on the project all along and has been biding his time, looking for a way. I warned you!'

She snapped her fingers impatiently. 'Never mind that. Get on with your story.'

'That's what I was coming to. He somehow found out we were having trouble with our steel suppliers and saw a way to throw a spanner in the works. By suggesting that we buy from the importers he was in league with, he could slow us down until we were forced to call in his company to bail us out.'

To Drew, it wasn't making much sense. 'How could finding us a cheaper supplier slow us down?'

'The price was just bait to get us to go along. He knew we'd find out that the stuff was substandard but by that time, the steel would have been delivered. We wouldn't be able to use it so there'd be a delay and extra costs in replacing it.'

'Which was exactly what had happened,' Drew confirmed. She didn't want to believe Garth's story. It was so much at odds with what she knew about Traig Monroe. And yet, there was the evidence of the steel itself. . . . . 'How did they get your co-operation?' she asked suddenly.

Garth twisted uncomfortably in his seat. 'You'll find out anyway so I've got nothing to lose by telling you now. They paid me to order from their supplier.'

She felt as if her feet had been cut out from under her. First Traig and now Garth, both supposedly working for her but working against her all along. 'You know what this means?' she asked Garth.

His expression was cold and unemotional, hiding the turmoil she was sure he must be feeling. 'I know.

It's the end of my job here. I knew this would happen as soon as Monroe appeared on the scene.'

Was she playing into Traig's hands if she dismissed Garth? He *had* predicted it, and without Garth she would have almost no chance of finishing Pacific Centre on time. 'Not necessarily,' she said slowly. 'If you can prove that Monroe was behind this, it may let us out of the consultant's clause. I could take the whole thing to the awards council. They would never allow Monroe's to take over if they had been the cause of the delay.' She studied Garth earnestly. '*Can* you prove it?'

She couldn't help thinking that Garth looked less like a man on the verge of a reprieve and more like one who had just been hoist by his own petard. Then his head came up and he squared his shoulders. 'I can prove it. I'll have the evidence on your desk first thing in the morning.'

After Garth had gone she stared at the office walls for a long time. She felt drained of emotion. She had been so close to telling Traig that she loved him and was ready to do anything to resolve their differences.

What a blessing it was that she hadn't made the call! She would have made herself look more of a fool than she was already. How Traig must be laughing at her now. He had helped solve the strike to blind her to his real intention, which was to gain control of Pacific Centre. Why else would he have bribed Garth to buy the faulty steel?

Of course, she only had Garth's word that Traig was behind it, and he had plenty of reason to hate Traig. But Garth had said he could prove his statement and would produce the evidence for her tomorrow.

She was also puzzled about why Traig would approach Garth, of all people, to carry out his scheme.

As far as she knew, the two men were barely on speaking terms. Unless the story about the plans being stolen was true—and Traig was blackmailing Garth. She shivered. It seemed the most likely explanation, although it didn't agree with what she knew of Traig's character.

But then, what did she really know about him? He was independent enough to want to make his own way in life, only claiming his inheritance when it was forced upon him. He was caring—that much she knew from seeing how he behaved towards his dying father. And he exerted a powerful physical attraction which she had mistaken for love.

She also knew he was ruthless enough to try to use her to prove his claim that Garth had stolen his plans. It added up to a powerful, complex personality capable of almost anything. How could she be sure he wouldn't stoop to using Garth to gain control of Pacific Centre? On the evidence, it seemed more than a possibility.

To her surprise, Traig was at home when she got there. She had been hoping he would still be at the hospital with his father. But he came out of the kitchen, wiping floury hands on a tea towel. 'It looks as if I timed everything just right,' he said when he saw her.

'You bet you did,' she said bitterly. At the sight of him, her senses had reacted independently of her mind, thrilling to an awareness of the strength of his lean, hard body and remembering how it felt to be crushed against that hardness and invaded by it. She would give anything to be back on the island with him. Or rather, with Christopher, their two rival companies far away and only their complementary physical needs to be considered.

He frowned. 'What do you mean by that?'

'I mean I found out that you bribed Garth Dangerfield to order substandard steel from your importer to jeopardise Pacific Centre.'

His welcoming expression was replaced by a coldness which repelled her. 'Is that what he told you?'

Devoid of emotion now, she nodded. 'He said you wouldn't be happy until you got him fired the way you did when he was working for your father.'

'Would it help if I said I don't know what the hell you're talking about?'

It was the one thing she wanted to hear more than anything in the world. But Garth had been so positive, and he had said he had evidence which proved Traig's involvement. Her doubts must have shown on her face because he said flatly, 'I can see that you don't believe me.'

'What else do you expect?' she flung at him. 'You've done nothing but deceive me from the moment we met.'

'I can't deny that. But I explained my reasons.'

Couldn't he see that his reasons weren't enough to justify him causing such havoc in her life? 'Your reasons—that's all that matters, isn't it? Never mind what anyone else thinks or feels. For some reason, you've got this insane vendetta going against Garth Dangerfield and I'm tired of being caught in the middle.'

'I have a very good reason for disliking Garth, too.'

She didn't want to hear it, whatever it was. 'I can't take any more lies,' she said huskily, tears constricting her throat. She put her hands over her ears to shut out his excuses.

Irresistibly, he forced her hands away from her ears, using his greater strength to pull her arms down to her sides where he pinned them. 'No lies, this time,' he promised. 'Garth Dangerfield was fired from Monroe's because he was using the firm for his own gain, manipulating Dad into the bargain. Once he left the company, that was the end of it as far as I was concerned, until I found out about the plans. So there's no vendetta against him, as you put it. I really only have one thing against Dangerfield now.'

'What's that?' she asked, although she was afraid she already knew the answer.

'You,' he said simply. 'When I saw you with him at the restaurant the other night, I could have strangled him with my bare hands.'

He still held her arms pinned but she lifted her head defiantly. 'Why? Because he dared to touch what you regarded as your property?'

'No, not property. But I did think we had something good together on the island. Damn it, I know we had.'

'That was between Drew and Christopher,' she reminded him. 'It's different now. This is between Traig and Miss Dominick.'

'It doesn't have to be different. If Drew and Christopher can manage to get along, surely Traig and Miss Dominick can. I love you, you know.'

It was the first time he had said it in so many words. Oh, he had said it with his body every time they made love on the island and when she had asked him, but now, hearing him spell it out, made her heart turn somersaults. 'I love you too,' she confessed. 'I think I have almost since we met.'

'My darling Drew.' He released her arms but only to imprison them more tightly in the force of a powerful embrace which drove the breath from her body. He started to kiss her hungrily but she resisted the urge to succumb and twisted away from him. He looked puzzled. 'What's the matter?'

'Now we know we both feel the same way, we have to talk,' she said urgently. 'And I can't even think straight when you hold me like this.'

'That's the idea,' he said warmly but reluctantly, he let her go. While she curled up in an armchair across the room, he walked unsteadily to the bar and mixed martinis for them both, then handed her one.

'Why would Garth say you had put him up to ordering the inferior steel?' she asked when he was seated opposite her.

He took a long pull on his drink. 'Isn't it obvious? He can see how things are between you and me and he'll do anything he can to blacken me in your eyes.'

Garth had said much the same thing about Traig, she recalled miserably. 'You can't deny that you came here hoping to find evidence to discredit me,' she reminded him.

'Not to discredit you—to establish the truth. I still intend to do that if I can.'

'Even if I get hurt?'

'I hope it won't come to that,' he said evenly. 'But I can't guarantee it.'

In that statement, she had her answer. Traig valued truth and justice more than his relationship with her. 'I see,' she said dully.

'You see what?' he demanded at once.

'Where I stand with you.'

'We weren't discussing that,' he said bleakly.

'Weren't we? You've just said you'll stop at nothing to establish the truth about Pacific Centre, even if it means hurting me. So how can I be sure you wouldn't also sell us poor quality materials to harm the project?'

'Because I damned well told you I didn't!' he exploded. For a frightening instant, she thought he was going to hit her, so fiercely evident was his rage.

He crossed the room in two strides and towered over her. Then he grasped her upper arms and hauled her to her feet. The suddenness of the movement made the room spin around her and she slumped against him for support. It was all he needed to pull her closer.

This time she did succumb to his kiss, feeling the graze of his moustache against her upper lip a fraction of a second before his lips ground against hers, Then the musky scent of his aftershave clogged her nostrils and his hand pressed into the small of her back, forcing her body to mould to his.

His need of her was all too evident and the realisation of it aroused a feverish response in her own body. Unwittingly, her response to his kiss became deeper and more passionate until there was no way she could hide her feelings from him.

Only when he steered her backwards towards the couch, did a small spark of resistance flare within her. 'No! This isn't the way,' she implored.

'It's the only way,' he assured her. He urged her backwards and down onto the soft cushions, then covered her body with his while his lips continued to coax more and more response from her mouth.

She was drowning in the sea of sensation he was creating within her. She was a violin and he was a virtuoso, his caresses as irresistible as the movement of bow against string. What chance did she have to fight him when he used weapons such as these?

Nevertheless, reason still ruled in some part of her mind and she struggled to surface from the drug of his passion. 'Traig, listen to me.'

He braced himself on his elbows so he was looking down at her, his face only inches away and his eyes cloudy with desire. 'I'm listening, but you'd better make it fast.'

'Garth says he has evidence to prove you were behind the shipment of faulty steel.'

He frowned. 'You find that nonsense important enough to interrupt our lovemaking?'

'But it's important to me,' she protested.

At once, he eased his weight off her and swung his legs down to the floor but remained seated on the edge of the couch next to her. 'In that case, it's important to me, too,' he said.

He raked a hand through his thick chestnut thatch, tousling it so he looked boyish and vulnerable as he had on the island. 'Hell, Drew, I wasn't trying to take advantage of you just now, if that's what you're thinking. I thought, perhaps, if we made love you would realise that I care too much about you ever to cheat you.'

'I know.' She ran a hand down his forearm, feeling the fine hairs rustle beneath her fingers. The aching sense of longing the contact imparted made her wish she hadn't stopped him. 'I feel the same way but I'm so confused about everything—us, Garth, Pacific Centre. It's all so mixed up.'

'We can't change what we are,' he said heavily. 'If we could, we might not feel the same way about each other.'

She was sure she would have felt the same way about him if he'd been a wharf labourer or door-to-door salesman. But she also knew that wasn't what he meant. He was referring to their strong personalities and the historical accident which made them rivals, no matter what they did. 'Traig. . . .' she began but he forestalled her.

'Let me say this. If I did have any quarrel with you I'd confront you with it fairly, not try to get my own back by underhanded methods.

'I know you have a different impression of me but I

value honesty and loyalty above most other qualities. Coming here as your employee was the only way I could get to see you. If there'd been another way, I'd have tried it. As it was, I would have told you the truth much sooner if . . . if I hadn't gone and fallen in love with you.'

She placed a finger across his lips to silence him. 'We've been through all that and I've already accepted your explanation. For the life of me, I don't know why I should—but I also believe that you're an honest man.'

'Thank you for that, at least. I only brought it up again to make you understand that as long as I'm in your employ, you will get only honesty and loyalty from me. Now it's up to you to decide who you're going to trust.'

In her mind, there was no contest. 'I trust you,' she conceded.

His relief was plain in the shining glance he turned on her. 'Thank God. So what will you do about Dangerfield?'

'I hadn't thought that far ahead. I'm seeing him tomorrow so I'll have it out with him then.'

'Whatever so-called proof he has to connect me with the steel shipment is bound to be forged,' he warned her.

'I know that now.' All the same she couldn't quite dismiss the feeling of unease which had haunted her since Garth told her about his 'evidence'.

With a forefinger, Traig traced the worry lines creasing her brow. 'You're still not a hundred per cent convinced, are you?' he asked.

She forced herself to smile, banishing the lines. 'Of course I am.'

At once, he leaned towards her, the heat radiating from his body penetrating her clothes.

'What are you doing?' she demanded.

'I told you I always finish what I start,' he said and claimed her mouth in a demanding kiss which left her in no doubt of what he meant.

When Traig held her and made love to her she had no doubts left. It was only afterwards, when she lay alone in the darkness of her own room, that her uncertainty returned. She had meant it when she told Traig she trusted him. If only Garth hadn't been so sure of himself.

The evidence he planned to show her in the morning must be forged. So why was she tossing and turning with worry over what tomorrow's meeting would uncover?

CHAPTER EIGHT

FOR the first time since she took control of the company, Drew was tempted to call Maggie and tell her she was too ill to come in to the office.

In a way, it was true. The very thought of the meeting with Garth this morning made her feel ill. He couldn't prove that Traig was connected with the steel shipment, since she had Traig's word that he was innocent. But the meeting would still be unpleasant, given the way she knew Garth felt about her.

Even Traig's presence across the table from her at breakfast couldn't bolster her flagging spirits. She refused his offer of scrambled egg and French toast. 'It looks delicious, but I'm not hungry right now.'

He eyed her keenly, his gaze caressing, reminding her of what they had shared last night. 'Would you like me to come with you?'

Decisively, she shook her head. 'Thanks for the offer, but no. Dad always taught me to do my own dirty work.'

'But you are not your father,' he said.

'I know. But I still feel I have to live up to his standards.'

'His standards may have been right for him. Are you sure they're right for you?'

She shrugged. 'They're the only ones I've ever known.'

His warm gaze slid over her slim curves which were evident even under the rather severe grey suit she'd chosen for this morning's meeting. 'Your father wasn't a woman, either.'

She laughed. 'That's about the last excuse Dad would have accepted from me.'

Traig reached across and grasped her hand, warming it with his body heat. 'It's not an excuse,' he said seriously, 'it's a fact of life.'

This time her answering laughter sounded more strained. 'You're not going to give me that old saw about choosing between having a career and being a woman, I hope?' She had expected more from him.

'Actually, I was going to remind you that you can be both. At the moment, career seems to be ahead on points.' He hesitated for a moment, weighing his words carefully. 'You can't replace Andrew Dominick, you know.'

'Nobody can do that,' she agreed, 'even though I carry most of his name. If I'd been a boy I would have been Andrew Dominick the second. Drew was the closest they could come for a girl.'

He poured more coffee for them both and pushed a cup across to her. 'Did it bother you, knowing you had disappointed your father by being a girl?'

'Of course not,' she said a shade too quickly, then added, 'all right, it did. I suppose that's why I've spent so much of my life trying to compensate for it.' Unaccountably, she was disturbed by the direction their conversation was taking, so she grinned cheekily. 'When did you take up psychology, Doctor Monroe?'

He smiled back, playing her game of 'everything's fine' but she guessed he wasn't fooled. 'Since I met you, Drew Dominick,' he answered. 'I have this tremendous urge to know what makes you tick.'

'Well I also tock and chime the hour,' she said flippantly, afraid to let him see how close to the real Drew he was getting. His probing, however well-meaning, was taking her into territory she preferred not to explore. She scrambled to her feet. 'Speaking of chiming the hour, it's time I was on my way.'

'You're sure you don't want me to come with you?'

'Absolutely. But thanks anyway.'

All the same as she drove to the office she wished he had been able to accompany her. His presence would have been comforting and he might have tamed a few of the butterflies which were holding a convention in her stomach. Despite her repeated assurances to Traig that she could handle the meeting, she hated unpleasantness and was not looking forward to the confrontation with Garth.

'How did it go yesterday?' Maggie asked after the lift deposited Drew at the Ivory Tower.

'How did what go?'

'You were going to call a truce between you and Traig Monroe,' Maggie prompted.

In the drama surrounding the steel delivery, Drew had forgotten all about that. It would have been so easy last night when they had already got as far as a declaration of love. But she had let Garth's accusations overshadow everything else.

She realised that Maggie didn't know about the faulty steel so she explained the details to her, leaving out Garth's part in it and his attempt to pin the blame on Traig.

Maggie whistled softly. 'I see. So that's what kept you here so late last night.'

'And also why straightening out my love life had to wait,' Drew added.

Maggie frowned. 'Just don't let it wait too long, that's all.'

In the privacy of her own office, Drew picked up the batch of mail Maggie had left on her desk, and curled up on the window seat to go through it. But the letters were quickly forgotten as she stared out at the city skyline. She hadn't been entirely honest with Maggie. She *could* have told Traig about the proposed truce between them—last night would have been the perfect time. Instead, she had let herself be overcome by his physical attraction so they still hadn't talked about the future or how they were going to resolve their differences, both personal and professional.

Assuming they *had* a future together, she thought bleakly. Perhaps she was taking too much for granted in thinking that he wanted to marry her. He had said he loved her and they knew they could live happily under the same roof—the last few weeks proved that. But how would she feel if that was enough for him? She might be old fashioned, but it wasn't enough for her. She wanted the same kind of commitment which had prevented her father from marrying again, rather than betray the memory of the woman he had loved and lost.

Was she being too idealistic? Maybe. But she knew that, for her, there was no other way.

Just then, the sun which had been hiding behind a canopy of grey clouds, emerged to bathe her in golden light. It shone like a beacon down the chasm created by the tall office buildings.

She smiled up at the sunbeams dancing across her face. 'Thank you, sun,' she said happily. Whether it was a sign or not, she couldn't have said, but there was nothing to say she couldn't treat it as one. She and Traig would work things out somehow.

Her intercom buzzed, startling her. Gracefully, she uncurled from the window seat and reached across her desk to answer it. 'Yes, Maggie?'

'Mr Dangerfield is here to see you,' came Maggie's distorted voice through the speaker.

The spark of joy which the sunbeams had lit in her was quickly extinguished by apprehension. 'Just a minute,' she said and slid behind her desk, folding her hands primly in front of her. 'Ask him to come in.'

At once the door opened and Garth came in. He seemed to have aged since last night, and dark shadows rimmed his eyes. He was wearing the same suit he'd had on the previous night and it was rumpled, suggesting that he'd slept in his clothes. Well, he would soon find out his sleepless night had been justified.

Wordlessly he placed a manilla folder on her desk and stepped back.

She waved him towards a chair. 'Have a seat, Garth.'

He hesitated as if about to defend his right to stand, then shrugged and slumped into the chair, his eyes never leaving the manilla folder.

Deliberately, Drew ignored the folder and faced Garth across the desk. 'Traig Monroe denies having anything to do with the steel shipment,' she said briskly and waited for his reaction.

His eyes, hooded until then, flickered to her face and she was chilled by the unrelenting hatred she saw in them. 'He would say that,' he snarled, 'but that's the way the Monroes do things. They get you out on a limb and then saw it off.' His lips twisted into a bitter parody of a smile. 'You should know that better than anybody.'

He was referring to the way Darcy Monroe had inveigled her father into the ill-fated deal which began their feud. As soon as Andrew Dominick's resources were committed to the deal, Darcy had backed out. 'What's past is past,' she said firmly. 'It has nothing to do with this situation.'

'Doesn't it?' Garth asked nastily. 'There's a pattern here, whether you admit it or not. Monroe has managed to get you to fall for him. Don't bother to deny it,' he said when she made a move to interrupt, 'I haven't stood a chance since the day he turned up.

'But mark my words. Now he's got you committed to him, he'll leave you high and dry like his father did to yours, and he's now trying to do to me. Except that he isn't getting away with it this time.'

Drew schooled her features into an impassive mask, determined not to let Garth see how badly his prediction had shaken her. It was too close to what she had been thinking earlier. 'You said you had proof that Traig was involved in the steel purchase,' she prompted.

He folded his arms and sat back. 'It's all in that folder.'

'I'd prefer you to explain it to me,' she said, resisting the urge to reach for the folder herself.

Grudgingly, Garth stood up and moved over to her desk, then opened the folder and fanned the contents out in front of her. 'Exhibit A,' he said, placing a typewritten letter on top. It was addressed to Garth and was dated a few weeks previously. The letterhead belonged to the importer whose steel had turned out to be faulty.

'What does this prove?' she asked coldly, determined not to make this easy for him. He thought Traig would be the victim but he still couldn't see that he was only making things look blacker for himself.

'Why don't you read the letter, Miss Dominick,' he said, using her name as if it was an insult.

Quickly, she scanned the single-page letter. It confirmed arrangements made earlier for the delivery of the steel between Dominick's . . . 'and Mr Monroe of your organisation'.

The rest of the typescript blurred before her eyes and she drew a painful breath. Then she recalled Traig's warning that Garth would stop at nothing to discredit him, even if it meant forging the 'proof' he needed.

'How do I know this is genuine?' she asked Garth.

'You don't,' he said unexpectedly. 'Although there are more letters like that in the folder. But you have to believe this.'

He thrust a cheque in front of her face. It was for a large amount and was made out in favour of G. Dangerfield. The signature was that of C. Traig Monroe. 'This could be forged, too,' she said shakily, striving to keep the tremor out of her voice.

'Of course it could, but it isn't. You can check the signature for yourself.'

She was tempted to refuse outright but for the sake of justice, she had to give Garth this final benefit of the doubt. Reluctantly, she reached into her desk and brought out some of the paperwork Traig had prepared for her party. His signature was at the bottom of one sheet. She lined it up alongside the cheque and could no longer ignore the damning evidence of her own eyes.

The signatures were identical.

'I see you're getting the message,' Garth said as he watched her calm expression give way to a horror she was unable to conceal.

'This cheque could be for anything,' she said, clutching at straws.

'You know how friendly I am with Mr Monroe,' Garth drawled. 'Why would he send me money if it wasn't to buy my co-operation on this deal? You know what it means to him.'

He was right. There was no reason why he should possess a cheque made out in his favour by Traig, unless it was for the purpose he stated. There was only one possible conclusion. Traig had lied to her. Even while he was telling her how much he valued honesty, he had been twisting the truth to suit himself.

She felt sick as she recalled what she had let him do next. Believing him, she had given herself to him trustingly, and all the time he must have been laughing at her for being so gullible.

'This doesn't change the fact that you accepted money to act against the best interests of this company,' she said icily, thinking bitterly, 'the show must go on'.

Anger flared in Garth's face, banishing the triumph which had been there a moment before. 'Now just a minute, I told you I didn't know the material was substandard. I thought I was doing you a good turn.'

'And what do you call this?' she demanded, waving the cheque at him.

'Commission,' he said defiantly.

It was no use. He just couldn't see that his action was every bit as despicable as ... as Traig's. At least in the feud between their families, Traig had a reason for what he did, she thought with bitter irony. He always seemed to have a good reason for hurting her.

Garth was watching her intently. 'It's all right for you,' he spat at her, 'you were born with a silver spoon in your mouth. You wouldn't understand why a man would try to make a bit extra on the side, because you never had to. You can afford to be so high and mighty.'

'Stop it!' she commanded sharply. 'We're not discussing my actions here. The fact remains that what you did was totally unethical, no matter how you try to justify it. Under the circumstances, I don't see how we can go on working together.'

'That's about what I expected,' he snarled. 'Don't worry, I'll leave quietly. But I don't know how much consolation wonder boy will be to you now you know his true colours.'

Bleakly, Drew asked herself the same thing. But she wasn't going to give Garth the satisfaction of admitting it. She reached for the phone. 'I'll have Personnel make up your severance pay. You can leave today.'

He doffed an imaginary hat at her. 'It will be a pleasure.'

He picked up the folder from her desk, slid the papers and the damning cheque back into it and started for the door. Before he reached it, she put down the phone. 'There's one more thing, Garth.'

He half-turned. 'What?'

'The original designs for Pacific Centre—they were stolen from Traig Monroe, weren't they?'

He stared at her, all the love he'd professed to feel for her now turned into loathing. 'You had to have your pound of flesh, didn't you?'

She refused to be goaded. 'Answer me, Garth, or I'll see that you never again work on a building project in Sydney.'

He shrugged. 'I wasn't planning to. As they used to say in the wild west, this city isn't big enough for both me and Monroe. So I suppose it doesn't matter if you know it all. Yes, Monroe drew up the first set of plans for the Centre. But I added a lot of my own ideas later, so it wasn't all his work.'

Feeling suddenly weary, she pressed a hand to each side of her forehead. 'Get out of here.'

As soon as the door closed behind him, she dialled the Personnel Manager and instructed him to pay Garth off. Then she slumped in her chair. What in the name of Heaven was she to do now?

The award she had worked so hard for had been won under false pretences. The project which had been her pride and joy was the result of a stolen idea. No wonder Traig couldn't pass the site without hating her. In his position, she would have felt the same way. Which still didn't excuse the fact that he had tried to sabotage the project. She could have forgiven him for that, come to think of it, perhaps even forgiven him for bribing Garth to buy the substandard steel—but she couldn't forgive him for lying to her about his part in it.

Worse, he had taken her to bed with him on the strength of that misplaced trust, she thought. Damn him! She should have listened to her father. He had said you couldn't trust a Monroe. But then, he had never fallen in love with one.

She closed her eyes and rested her head on her folded arms on the desk, too drained even to cry. Her head throbbed unbearably. If only she'd never started this wife business she would never have got to know Traig Monroe. He would probably have found some other way to get his revenge for the stolen plans, she guessed. It was just bad luck that he'd been standing in Colleen Bell's office when Drew called asking her to hire someone to run her life.

Run it—or ruin it? she thought miserably. He had managed to do both. The question was, what was she to do about it?

He would have to be told about Garth's confession, of course. How he would gloat then. She sighed unhappily. There was no point in putting it off. She lifted her head and reached for the telephone.

He answered on the third ring. 'Dominick residence.'

'It's Drew.'

He broke in before she could continue. 'Darling! How did the meeting with Dangerfield go? I've been worrying since you left.'

'I'll bet you have,' she thought grimly. Worried in case Garth managed to implicate him, most likely.

Aloud she said, 'The meeting is over. I learned what I needed to know. Can you come to the office and talk about it?'

'From the way you sound, it must have been hell. I have to go and visit Dad this afternoon so I'll call in on my way. Will that be soon enough?'

'It will have to do,' she said flatly and hung up before he could say any more.

A glance at her clock told her it was still mid-morning. Somehow she had to get through the hours before Traig came. It was the second time in one day that she had cause to dread a meeting and it was too much!

'Work cures all ills,' had been one of her father's maxims. Deciding to test his theory, she plunged into the pile of paperwork on her desk, attacking it with a ruthlessness she hadn't known she possessed.

Heaven help anyone unfortunate enough to seek charity from the company this morning. In her present frame of mind it was much easier to say no than yes, she found as she vetoed yet another request, leaving it to Maggie to turn it into a polite refusal.

Then she decided she wasn't being fair to the charities who had written seeking her company's help, and pushed the letters aside to deal with some other time. They weren't to blame for the acute sense of betrayal she was feeling. And it wasn't Garth who was responsible for it, either. She knew now that she hadn't really expected him to behave differently. Somehow, she had sensed that she couldn't trust him, which accounted for her reluctance to become involved with him. He had seemed talented and she had felt sorry for him when he told her how he had been pushed out of Monroe's. Her faith in him had seemed to be vindicated when the company won the award with his design. If only it had been his design, she thought ruefully.

Just before one, Maggie breezed in and asked Drew to join her for lunch in the executive dining room. 'It's roast veal, must be somebody's birthday,' she joked.

'No thanks, Maggie, I'm not hungry,' Drew demurred.

'Take-away food last night, not hungry today—you *must* be in love,' Maggie surmised.

Drew's eyes flashed fire as they met her assistant's. 'That was last night,' she said fiercely.

Maggie's eyebrows tilted upwards. 'Like that is it! Ah well, they say the course of true love never does run smoothly.'

How right 'they' were, Drew told herself after Maggie went off to lunch. It was even worse in her case. The course of true love had reached a dead end.

She was still contemplating this grim fact when a sound from her outer office caught her attention. Maggie must have forgotten something. She flicked the intercom switch. 'Maggie, is that you?'

There was a pause then a male voice answered, 'If it is, she's grown a moustache.'

Her heart sank. Only yesterday she would have given him a laughing response, then run to the door and thrown herself into his arms. Today, she felt frozen to her chair. 'Come in, Traig,' she said dully.

Even while her mind was listing all the reasons she had to hate him, her body reacted to his nearness in its own way. Try as she might, she couldn't subdue or ignore the fiery sensation which tore through her veins at the sight of him standing in her office doorway.

He filled two-thirds of the opening and leaned against one jamb, that slightly crooked smile knocking all her pre-rehearsed accusations out of her head.

She ached to run her hands through his thatch of

chestnut hair which was windblown from the street, and mould herself against the lean hard contours of his body. But she remained where she was, observing these sensations as if they belonged to someone else. He was the enemy. You only loved your enemy in parables, not real life.

'Come in and close the door,' she said, marvelling that she was able to sound so controlled, given the turmoil raging inside her.

He did as bidden, relaxing into a visitor's chair with the grace of a panther settling into its lair. 'That's not much of a welcome,' he said warily.

She came to life at last. 'What did you expect? Bells and drums?'

'I suppose not. I know you've had a rough morning.'

'Don't humour me!' she snapped. 'But then you, of all people, would have known how rough it was going to be. What was last night—the softening up?'

He jerked upright, bracing himself against her desk with both palms flat against the timber surface, as if he was going to spring at her like the panther she'd been comparing him to. 'That's a hell of a thing to say!'

He was hurt and confused by her attitude, she could see that. But she'd been hurt and confused, too. So much that she was driven by the urge to hurt back. 'Why don't we both stop pretending,' she said tiredly. 'I got the whole story from Garth Dangerfield this morning.'

'I warned you he'd stop at nothing. But I didn't expect him to be able to convince you. Whatever he said. . . .'

'He didn't *say* anything,' she interrupted in the same tired tone. 'He showed me the cheque you gave him for buying the steel from your supplier. I checked the signature—it was yours all right.'

It was hard to believe he was faking his air of injured innocence. 'Cheque? But I don't . . . oh, hell!'

'Then you did give him a cheque?' she asked, noting the dawning awareness in his expression.

'Yes, I did. But not to bribe him to betray you.'

'Then what was it, severance pay?' she asked sarcastically, unable to hide her disbelief.

Distractedly he raked his fingers through his hair. 'As a matter of fact, it was something like that. Monroe's owed him a sum of money he'd contributed to the superannuation fund. It was overlooked when he left. The computer. . . .'

'That was nearly two years ago,' she cut in. 'Come on, Traig, you may have been able to fool me at first, but I'm starting to understand you. For someone who is supposed to value honesty, you're very good at twisting the truth to suit yourself.'

'Then there's no way I can convince you I had nothing to do with the faulty steel?' he asked coldly.

'No, I'm sorry.'

He stood up slowly. 'Don't be sorry. Be glad you found out in time how you really feel about me.'

If he only knew how she really felt about him, she thought miserably. Despite everything, she still loved him and probably always would. But she couldn't trust him, that much was plain, so it was better to end it now before she got hurt. That was, hurt more than she was already, she amended privately.

He had started for the door when she stopped him. 'Wait, there's something else we have to discuss.'

'I thought we'd said everything that needed saying,' he rejoined, but stopped where he was.

'Garth confessed to stealing your design for Pacific Centre and passing it off as his own work,' she explained.

'I see.'

'Aren't you going to say "I told you so"?' she asked.

He came back and sat down again. 'I could, but in this case, being proved right gives me no satisfaction, although I don't expect you to believe that.'

Ignoring this, she went on, 'Of course I'll see the judges and arrange to return the award as soon as possible.'

'That would mean handing over completion of the project to Monroe Investments.'

Without looking at him, she nodded, feeling tears prick the backs of her eyes. 'Isn't that what you wanted all along?' she asked huskily.

'No, damn it, it isn't!' His closed fist came crashing down on the desk top with a force which rattled her pens and startled her into looking up at him.

'Then what *do* you want from me?' she asked, bewildered.

He thought for a moment. 'Handing the award back would only make the judges feel foolish and damage the reputations of both our companies. There's another solution.'

A tremor passed through her. All he was worried about was how his company would look if the truth came out. Dominick's would get the worst of it, of course, but the scandal would hurt both companies in the long run. So he was trying to protect himself, more than her. 'What do you suggest?' she asked.

'I suggest you invoke the consultant's clause right away. That would bring my company in as co-developers. With Garth out of the picture, you're going to need someone to take over. That will be me.'

She looked at him in amazement. 'You would do that for me?'

'Not for you, for both of us,' he amended.

'But Dominick's will still get the credit for the design,' she pointed out. 'That's hardly fair since it was your idea.'

'Life isn't fair,' he said shortly. 'In any case, you and Garth have changed some aspects of the design, enough to claim at least some of the credit.'

She hadn't thought of it like that. 'I suppose that's true,' she agreed.

'Besides which, I've told you I'm not after glory. I just wanted to see justice done. It made me sick thinking about Dangerfield strutting around like a peacock, building his reputation on the strength of my work.'

And thinking about Dangerfield taking her out? she wondered, feeling a thrill course through her. Could he have been jealous of Garth as well as worrying about the project? Then she reminded herself she would have to stop thinking like that. Her relationship with Traig was fated to continue, it seemed, but after today they could never go back to the closeness they had shared.

Warm colour rushed to her cheeks as she recalled last night. He had been so gentle but persuasive, she remembered. Had it all been a lie, designed to keep her off-guard and blind to his real purpose?

'This doesn't change how I feel about you,' he said, breaking into her thoughts.

Could he read her mind, too? 'Maybe it doesn't,' she said defensively, 'but it changes how *I* feel. We can't go on living under the same roof after this.'

'No, I suppose we can't.'

Damn him, why didn't he argue, fight, resist? Why was he so iron-hard when it came to business and so compliant where she was concerned? Couldn't he see that it would take so little to make her beg him to stay? Instead, she heard herself say aloud, 'Your contract is almost up anyway. Why don't you leave right away?'

'If that's the way you want it.'

No, it wasn't the way she wanted it, her mind

screamed. It was the way it had to be. He had deceived her, betrayed her. How could she possibly still love him after that? She only knew that contrarily, she did.

'That's the way I want it,' she lied.

Almost instantly, he seemed to snap into another gear altogether. His mind began racing ahead to the challenge of completing Pacific Centre—his brainchild as much as hers now. 'We'll need to pull a few rabbits out of hats to replace the steel shipment,' he mused.

'I'm sure you'll think of something,' she said dryly. In this mood he reminded her of her father, who could also dismiss personal worries and concentrate solely on the job at hand. If only she had the same ability.

Making a determined effort, she brought her mind to bear on the problems facing the project. But all the time, she was conscious of the controlled strength of his lean fingers as they stabbed the air to make a point. The fire in his eyes was different from the one she had kindled there last night, but it was still compelling to see. And the angle of his body thrusting towards her made her stomach muscles tighten with awareness of him.

Stop it! she told herself severely. She was as much a business person as he was. If he could push their relationship out of his mind and get on with the job, then she would do the same if it killed her.

By the time she had brought him up to date on the progress of Pacific Centre before the steel problem arose, he was looking at her with a new respect. 'You really know your stuff, don't you?' he said admiringly.

Annoyance made her defensive. 'What did you expect, a partner who is as compliant on the job as she is in bed?'

An angry frown creased his forehead. 'I didn't deserve that,' he retorted. 'If you can't separate bedroom and boardroom, maybe it's just as well that I'm moving out right away.'

The frustration of having him so disturbingly near, yet so completely beyond her reach, snapped her remaining self-control. 'You really are the limit!' she exploded. 'You accuse *me* of confusing bedroom and boardroom, but you're the one who used my bedroom to get you where you are now.'

The muscles in his jaw worked convulsively and she was alarmed at how far she had dared to provoke him. 'So that's how you see it,' he said quietly, his voice throaty with controlled rage. 'How stupid of me to think I was doing you a favour by sparing your company a public scandal.'

She was beyond all reasoning now. 'Spare me? You were only doing it to keep your own company lily white.'

'We weren't the ones who stole the plans,' he reminded her.

'And neither did I,' she rejoined triumphantly.

'You're forgetting something.'

Her head came up defiantly. 'And what's that?'

'The old saying that the buck stops here. It's your company, so you have to take some of the blame for what happened.'

So it had finally come to that. He *did* hold her responsible for stealing his precious plans. Well, at least he was making it easier for her to get over him. Much more of this and there would be nothing left of the love she now felt for him.

He seemed to sense that he had gone too far. 'I'm sorry, Drew, I didn't mean to sound off at you like that.'

'As you pointed out before, maybe it's better if we find out in time how we really feel about each other,' she said stiffly.

He shook his head despairingly. 'I didn't mean it should come to this.'

'I think you'd better go.'

He nodded and left at once, leaving the office feeling more empty than it had ever done before. She wanted to call him back and beg him to forgive her, but she couldn't do it. There was too much hatred between their families and it had permeated both of them so they were incapable of seeing each other clearly or of judging each other fairly.

I hate him! she thought vehemently. Only then she remembered how thin was the dividing line between hate and love.

Her telephone shrilled but she remained where she was, unable to summon the physical resources to answer it. At last it's demanding ring pierced her torpor and she moved to the desk like a robot. 'Drew Dominick,' she said, and her voice sounded metallic and unreal to her ears.

'Miss Dominick, this is the Charge Sister at Sydney Hospital. Is Mr Traig Monroe with you?'

A sense of foreboding invaded her. 'He was but he just left. He said he was on his way to see you. Is . . . is something wrong?'

'I'm afraid there is. His father has had the second stroke we've been fearing. He may not recover this time.'

'Oh, God,' she breathed. 'Is there anything I can do?'

'As a matter of fact, there is. He was asking for you before he became unconscious. If he comes around it might help to have you here, to save him further distress.'

'Of course, I'll come right away. Is there anything else I can do to help?'

'Just hope that his son gets here in time.'

CHAPTER NINE

'HOPE that his son gets here in time.'

The words hammered at Drew's brain as she drove the short distance from her office to the hospital. She had decided to take her own car in case she was there for some time.

The traffic in the city centre seemed determined to hamper her progress. As she pulled up behind yet another obstruction, she forced herself to take deep, calming breaths.

'It's not your fault,' she told the strained face which looked back at her from the driving mirror. All the same, the eyes appraised her accusingly whenever she checked the mirror.

If only she hadn't kept Traig tied up with senseless quarrelling, he would have arrived at the hospital while Darcy was still conscious. Now he might never see his father again and she would be the one to blame.

It was a foolish notion, of course. She couldn't possibly have known what was going to happen. But it didn't prevent her from chiding herself over and over as she drove.

She was in a torment of guilt and self-condemnation by the time she reached the hospital where she was directed to the intensive care facility to which Darcy had been moved.

In the nearby waiting room, she found Traig slumped in a chair, his face grey. It was all she could do not to kneel at his side and wrap her arms around his shoulders. If only she could erase all that stood between them and be free to shield him with the force of her love.

He looked up as she entered, and the coldness in his expression warned her that any such gesture would be met with contempt. She was a Dominick and he had made it clear that he despised her.

'Don't say it, please,' she whispered. 'I know it was my fault that you didn't get here sooner.'

He stared at her in pained disbelief. 'I wasn't going to say that. If anything, I blame myself. I should have come straight here instead of letting other things get in the way.'

Other things—like her, for instance? But now wasn't the time to go into it. 'How is Darcy?' she asked.

'Dying,' he said tonelessly. 'If he'd managed to avoid the second stroke, he might have had a chance. He was told to take things quietly, not get excited. But as usual he wouldn't listen to advice. He was trying to write a letter, for God's sake!'

'Like my Dad,' she said thoughtfully. 'Business came first. He wouldn't listen to anybody, either. Maybe that's why our fathers didn't get along—they're too much alike.'

Like you and me, his answering glance seemed to say. But all he said was, 'Probably.'

Belatedly, he looked at her quizzically. 'What are you doing here, anyway?'

She explained about the phone call which had brought her to the hospital and the fact that Darcy had been asking for her.

'He must have remembered what he wanted to tell you,' he said.

She nodded. 'I wonder what it was.'

He shrugged. 'I don't know but it must be important to him.'

Now, she would probably never find out what it was, she thought despondently. If only she had made more of an effort to come and see him. Instead, she had let her work take precedence over the needs of another human being. What sort of soulless creature did that make her?

To her astonishment, Traig took her hand in his. 'It's natural to feel guilty at a time like this, but blaming yourself won't change anything.'

His kindness only made her condemn herself more strongly. She pulled her hand away and averted her eyes before he could see the tears welling in them.

Misinterpreting her reaction, he frowned angrily. 'For God's sake, Drew! Must you pull away from me as if I had the plague? Of course, I'm forgetting that you interpret any sign of affection on my part as sexual blackmail to get my own way.'

Wrapping her arms defensively about herself she swung back towards him. 'I didn't mean it that way at all.'

'You made it quite clear what you think of me,' he said harshly. 'I'm the one who used your bedroom as a stepping stone to the boardroom, remember?'

What had possessed her to say such a terrible thing? She had been hurt and angry over the way he had deceived her so she hadn't stopped to think before she spoke. Now she realised she wasn't being fair to either of them by assuming he had made love to her only out of ambition.

Before she could frame an apology, a nurse appeared at the entrance to the waiting room. 'You can see your father now,' she said.

Traig stood up quickly. 'Is he conscious?'

'He's drifting in and out. There's much more damage this time so you have to be prepared that he may not recognise you.'

With his back ramrod straight and his face set in an expressionless mask, Traig followed the nurse out of the waiting room.

Watching him go, Drew felt as if someone had twisted a knife inside her. There was so much she wanted to say to him but it was as if they spoke two different languages. She would never be able to separate personal and business ethics as efficiently as he seemed to do. One rule for the bedroom and one for the boardroom, she thought, mentally echoing his phrase. She was sure he meant every word he said when they made love. But she couldn't adjust to the other man he turned into in business.

He had been right when they were together on the island. Traig and Christopher were two different people who played by different rules. But he had been wrong about Drew and Miss Dominick. They were one and the same, with only one set of rules which had to serve for personal and business encounters.

She had no idea how long she sat in the waiting room, alone with such thoughts. It must have been a long time judging by the position of the sun beyond the window when Traig came back for her, but it seemed as if only minutes had passed.

'He's asking for you,' he said quietly.

Darcy was hardly recognisable as the tough, virile man he had been as he lay in the tangle of life-support equipment. His skin was the colour of parchment, tightly stretched over a gaunt frame and his breathing was barely discernable.

She thought he was unconscious, so still was he lying when she approached his bed. But when he sensed her presence his eyes drifted open and he smiled crookedly. 'Hello, Dominick.'

Startled, she reached for the hand which fluttered weakly on the bedclothes. She had expected his last vestiges of speech to have gone but, if anything, he spoke more clearly than before. A tremor shook her.

Was this his last, valiant attempt to communicate in this life?

'Garth,' he whispered urgently. 'Tell . . . Garth. . . .'

Puzzled, she glanced across at Traig but he shook his head. 'Tell him what?' she urged gently.

Darcy's face contorted with the effort of putting his thoughts into words. 'No . . . tell you . . . Garth. . . .' He paused to gather his strength and she waited tensely. After a long interval, he opened his eyes again. 'Garth . . . steal . . .' he began but his voice faded to a whisper and ended on a long hissing breath.

She felt the fingers slacken in her grip and looked at Traig in alarm. 'Darcy?'

At once, Darcy's doctor moved between them and released Drew's hand, gesturing for her to leave the room. As she started to move away, the doctor checked Darcy quickly then shook his head.

Drew clutched a hand to her mouth in silent anguish. She had never been so close to death before and was shaken. She was unaware that tears had begun to course down her cheeks until something splashed wetly on to her clenched hands.

She felt rather than heard the nurse urge her back to the sanctuary of the waiting room, leaving Traig to pay his final respects to his father. A cup of coffee was thrust into her hands but they shook so badly, she was forced to set the cup down to avoid spilling the contents.

'I have to leave you for a few minutes,' the nurse said, her voice reaching Drew from a great distance. 'Will you be all right?'

Like an automaton, Drew nodded. She wasn't sure why she felt so bereft. It wasn't as if she had been close to Darcy Monroe, having only met him here in this hospital.

If anything, she should be cheering his end, since she had been brought up to believe he was totally evil.

Now she was old enough to know better. He was a human being and she mourned him as such.

When her own father died, she had been in another part of the country so she hadn't been with him at the last—not like this. However, she did know firsthand how acutely the loss of one's sole surviving parent was felt and her heart went out to Traig. He was now as alone in the world as she was.

Calmer now, she picked up the coffee and nursed it, feeling the welcome warmth seep from the cup into her fingers. What had Darcy been trying so hard to tell her? 'Garth . . . steal,' he had said. Was he trying to tell her that Garth had stolen the plans? If so, it was tragic that she had been unable to tell him that she already knew about it, putting his mind at rest.

It was at rest now, she thought, feeling sadness settle around her like a mantle. And Garth had paid the price for his actions, so Darcy had distressed himself needlessly.

Traig came in briefly to tell her not to wait any longer as there was nothing more she could do. Hurt, she nodded and gathered up her things.

'Will you be coming home tonight?' she asked.

'No. I'll send someone for my possessions in a day or so. I'll take over Pacific Centre when I've straightened Dad's affairs out.'

'There's no hurry,' she assured him. 'Take all the time you need.'

He nodded agreement. Fractionally, a smile lightened his taut expression. 'It's a good thing ours wasn't a real marriage,' he mused, 'otherwise the separation wouldn't be as painless as this.'

What on earth made him think the separation was painless? she marvelled when he left her alone again. Perhaps it was, for him. For her, it had left emotional scars which would be painful for a long time to come.

If she had expected some change in Traig when he returned to work a short time later, she was in for a surprise. Outwardly, he showed no sign of the strain these last days must have been for him. And since their bitter quarrel in her office when she had accused him of using her to gain control of Pacific Centre, he gave her no clue to what he was feeling inside.

They could have been polite strangers instead of ex-lovers, she thought when he called at her office to discuss an aspect of the project. Traig was in full charge now—Christopher with all his warmth and tenderness might never have existed.

'What did you say?' she asked blankly, becoming aware that he was speaking to her.

'I asked what you thought of this change in the roof line,' he repeated.'

'Oh, uh . . . yes, of course,' she said quickly.

He sighed impatiently. 'You weren't listening, were you?'

'Of course I was,' she bluffed, feeling her cheeks flood with colour. 'All right, I wasn't. I was thinking of something else.'

'I can guess,' he said softly. For a moment, his expression softened and his caressing gaze swept her back to the moment when he first made love to her on the island. Her nerve endings throbbed at the memory of his touch and she felt a disturbing warmth in the pit of her stomach. Then he looked away and when he turned back to her all trace of softness was gone. 'Maybe I should come back some other time.'

Was she imagining it or was his tone tinged with regret? 'It's all right,' she said hastily, 'explain it to me again. I promise to pay attention this time.'

Patiently, he outlined the proposed change again

while she forced herself to keep her mind on the plans spread out on the desk between them. But it was difficult when her thoughts kept straying backwards to those other poignant moments they spent together when everything was so different from the present. When he bent over the plans to point out some special feature to her, she ached to close the small distance between them and feel his arms tight around her again. But the distance may as well have been measured in miles—it was just as unbridgeable.

Traig didn't seem to share her feelings. He had thrown himself into co-ordinating Pacific Centre with the single-mindedness she had begun to expect from him.

Fortunately, he had been able to pull his rabbits out of their hats and replace the faulty steel shipment. It was the least he could do, after the part he had played in the drama. Nevertheless, she was grateful for his help since she had been at her wit's end, trying to conjure up replacement materials in the short time available.

There had been a few raised eyebrows when she announced that he was taking over, and the news was reported with some relish in Inky Hedges' column, but the novelty soon wore off. Now, it was as if he had been in charge of the project all along.

Characteristically he was not content just to carry on where Garth left off. Based on his intimate understanding of the project, he had already made several small but important changes which improved the design so she had no hesitation in agreeing to make the change in the roof line which he proposed.

Their meeting concluded, he started to roll up the plans. 'You know, if we can keep up the present pace for another two weeks, we'll be back on schedule,' he said idly, as if commenting on the weather.

Wide-eyed, she stared at him and excitement gripped her. 'That's impossible.'

He grinned. 'Some of these changes have saved us time and we've gained more time by working on some of the other areas while waiting for the new steel to be delivered.'

'You're a miracle worker,' she said unhesitatingly.

He looked uncomfortable. 'I wish I was. But I only seem to be able to work my miracles where it matters the least to me.'

With that, he finished rolling the plans and left, giving her no chance to ask him what he meant by this comment.

She didn't have another chance to talk to him for some time because he seemed to be taking pains to keep out of her way. If a consultation was needed, he sent Kurt Wilder in his place. When she asked Kurt why Traig didn't come himself, he shrugged.

'I suppose he feels he's needed at the site.'

This gave her an idea. Why not visit the Pacific Centre site and see how things were going? She had deliberately kept away since Traig took over to demonstrate her confidence in him and avoid undermining his authority. Now that aim had been achieved, there was nothing to stop her inspecting the project.

Her sudden desire to visit the site had nothing to do with Traig or the fact that he hadn't spoken to her in over a week, she rationalised when she arrived at the site. She was merely curious to see how much progress had been made.

Stage one of the keyhole-shaped building was almost complete in appearance, although it was still only an outer shell. The interior finishes would not be added until much later.

This was the lowest of the sections which would

eventually comprise Pacific Centre, yet she still felt dwarfed by it as she stood looking upwards.

When it was finished, the centre would tower nearly seven hundred feet above sea level and would enclose half a million square feet of space.

The tower would be centred around a 'rainforest' courtyard with residential apartments on the upper floors, four podium levels, a four-storey department store, and a trade centre capable of accommodating 3,500 people. At street level, a variety of taverns, restaurants and shops would be grouped around small landscaped plazas.

'Impressive, isn't it?'

She turned to find Kurt Wilder standing behind her. 'It certainly is,' she agreed. 'It's one thing to see a project like this on paper and another to see it taking shape in reality.'

'That's what Andrew used to say,' he told her. 'He said it was like owning the biggest Meccano set in the world.'

Yet no child's construction set could have been responsible for the miracle taking place before them. It had seemed ambitous enough in the planning stages. Now she could see it rising around her, it took her breath away. But even as she toured the site, she was unconsciously looking for only one figure among the hundreds at work all around her.

At last her roving gaze located him among a group of men working on a network of girders high above the ground. His face was shadowed by the regulation hard hat he was wearing, but there was no mistaking the authority in his lean profile or the determination in his jut jaw. Her heart began to hammer painfully at the sight of him.

He finished giving his instructions then swung himself down off the framework with the agility of a circus performer, landing lightly on his feet some distance from her.

But before she could call out to him, he strode across the site to where a young woman was waiting. She was also wearing a hard hat, but even so Drew recognised her as the woman Traig had been dining with on the night he was called away to the hospital.

In broad daylight, she looked even more attractive than she had in the restaurant. Drew realised she was younger than she'd first thought, with a trim figure clad in stylish overalls over a striped sweater.

While Drew watched, Traig clasped an arm around the woman's shoulders and pulled her playfully against him. Then they strode off, arm-in-arm.

Shaken, Drew turned back to Kurt. 'Would you have my car brought around to the main entrance? I've seen enough.'

She'd seen a lot more than she bargained for, she thought miserably on her way back to her office. So that was why Traig was too busy to see her. He claimed to be in love with Drew but it hadn't taken him long to find consolation elsewhere.

It was hardly fair to blame him for turning to someone else, she told herself sternly. Drew had been the one to spurn him, so she had no further claim on his affections. Of all people, she should know that he was a normal man with strong, healthy drives so he was not likely to remain celibate for long.

All of which was logical and sensible so why did she feel as if someone had just torn her heart out by its roots? She had faced the fact that without trust between them, there could be no future in their relationship. Surely she wasn't so selfish that she would deny him happiness just because she would not be a part of it?

'There's an invitation on your desk,' Maggie told

her when she returned to her office. 'You won't believe what it's for.'

Normally, Maggie's comment would have aroused her own curiosity but today she didn't care if royalty had invited her to dinner. 'Whatever it is, I doubt if I'll be going,' she said tiredly.

Maggie grinned. 'I wouldn't bet on that.'

To satisfy her assistant who hovered expectantly in the doorway, Drew sat down at her desk and opened the envelope she found there. As Maggie had said, it was an invitation—to a memorial dinner being given by the building industry. 'In honour of Darcy Monroe,' she said in surprise. Traig was to be the guest of honour.

'I told you you wouldn't believe it,' Maggie crowed, satisfied that her surprise had achieved the desired impact. 'What your father would have said to see you getting an invitation like that. . . .'

It would never have happened while her father and Darcy still lived, she thought—more was the pity. If the two men had been able to resolve their differences, she and Traig would have had the chance to get to know each other free of the shadow of their parents' feud. Now, it was too late.

'I can't go,' she said flatly.

Maggie frowned. 'Traig might have something to say about that. I'm sure he will want you to be his escort.'

He wouldn't be pleased if she refused the invitation, she was sure. But not because he wanted her to go with him. After what she had seen at the building site, she expected he would ask his attractive friend to fill that role, as she had no doubt filled any other gaps Drew had left in his life.

'Besides which,' Maggie continued, 'I thought you liked the old man.'

'He reminded me a lot of Dad,' Drew confessed. 'I suppose it wouldn't hurt to pay him that much respect. Even Dad wouldn't argue about the rightness of my attending on these grounds.'

'Then I can tell the organisers that you accept?'

'I suppose so.' She looked at the invitation again. It was for Drew Dominick and associate. 'Tell them Kurt Wilder will be my escort,' she said on impulse. The old engineer would enjoy the evening among his peers in the industry, she imagined. He might be retired, but he clearly hadn't lost his eye for an attractive female, so he would probably get a kick out of being her escort.

What Inky Hedges would make of Kurt, she couldn't imagine, but she was beyond caring. She had been compared to her father in many ways. Now she could add one more. Just as he had been a one-woman man, she was a one-man woman. Even if they had no future together, that man was still Traig Monroe.

At the door, Maggie turned. 'I almost forgot, one of Darcy's doctors was on the phone for you.'

Drew's brow wrinkled prettily. 'A doctor? Did he leave a message?'

'He said Darcy gave him a letter for you. The doctor was supposed to delivery it but mislaid it then forgot about it until he came across it again.'

The idea of getting a letter from Darcy now, after his death, made her shiver. 'It's not more trouble, I hope. Is he bringing the letter here?'

'He said he would give it to you at the testimonial dinner.'

Drew's eyes narrowed with suspicion. 'What made him so sure I'd be there?' Then she caught Maggie's guilty expression. 'You knew all along that I wouldn't refuse, so you told him he could see me there.'

Maggie grinned disarmingly. 'What are good assistants for?'

'You mean what are assistants good for?' Drew retorted, but the affection in her voice took any sting out of the taunt.

All the same she was disturbed by Maggie's message. The idea of Darcy reaching out to her now was chilling, even though it was probably nothing. She made an effort to push it from her mind. She would find out soon enough.

As she had hoped, Kurt was delighted when she asked him to accompany her to the memorial dinner for Darcy Monroe. 'Are you sure you can trust yourself with me?' he asked impishly.

'Of course not. That's why I asked you,' she responded, knowing she'd made his day.

As soon as she replaced the receiver, the telephone rang again. She answered the wrong extension before she realised the call was coming through on her private line. In the act of reaching for it she froze, some instinct telling her that the caller was Traig.

It was an effort to pick up the phone. 'Yes?'

'Hello, Drew.' His voice, so velvety warm and caressing made her want to cry. You can't possibly be in love with a man you can't trust, she reminded herself. 'Are you there?' he repeated.

'Yes, I'm here.' I've been here all week while you've been amusing yourself with your new girl-friend, she added to herself. Such pettiness was so much out of character for her that she winced and made an effort to sound more reasonable. 'What can I do for you?'

'I saw you out at the site this morning but by the time I came looking for you, you'd gone.'

Calm and reasonable, she repeated to herself like a litany. 'It was only a flying visit to see how things are going,' she said in what she hoped was a bright, conversational tone.

'Oh. Then you didn't want to see me?'

Was she imagining the disappointment in his voice? 'Not particularly,' she said firmly, adding for good measure, 'but now I have you on the phone, the project is looking marvellous.'

'I'm glad you think so,' he said a little more coolly. 'But that wasn't why I called. Did you get my invitation?'

'I got one from the building industry group, to a testimonial dinner for Darcy,' she responded, puzzled. What did he mean by *his* invitation?

'They're hosting the dinner but I asked them to send you the invitation hoping you would agree to come as my guest.'

This time, there was no need for her to pretend disappointment. 'I didn't know. I've already accepted for myself and Kurt Wilding.'

She heard his quick indrawn breath. 'Kurt Wilding?' he repeated, his voice resonant with annoyance. 'You'd really rather go with him?'

'I naturally assumed you'd be going with your girlfriend,' she interposed calmly, although she was shaking with the effort of controlling her emotions.

It was his turn to sound puzzled. 'Girlfriend? What are you talking about?'

'The one I saw you with at the site this morning, and having dinner with you at the restaurant.'

'I still don't . . . oh, you must mean Louella.'

'Whatever,' she said, doing her best to sound offhand and not succeeding very well.

'Drew, Louella is my *sister*,' he explained in a tone of exasperation. 'She's also a nursing sister and had a lot to do with taking care of Dad during his last days. She lives in Darwin with her husband but she came down to Sydney to help look after Dad and be with him.'

'Your sister?' So all her jealous feelings had been for nothing. 'I didn't know.'

'Would it have made a difference if you had?'

She hesitated. Would it have made a difference? 'No,' she answered at last. Even though she was absurdly relieved that he hadn't turned to someone else so quickly, she couldn't alter the fact that he had betrayed her trust and would no doubt do it again.

'I see.' This time, the disappointment in his voice was unmistakable. 'You wouldn't change your mind I suppose?'

Was he referring to the dinner arrangements . . . or something else? It was easier to pretend he meant the former. 'I can't,' she said with genuine regret. 'I've already invited Kurt.'

'In that case, I'll see you both at the dinner.'

Suddenly, she felt an urgent need to prolong the contact just to hear his voice in her ear a moment or two longer. 'Traig. . . .' she began.

But he had already hung up.

Still, she would see him at the dinner, she consoled herself. She couldn't go on like this forever, she knew. Sooner or later, it would be better for them both if they went their separate ways. Working together like this only prolonged the agony. This time, the girl on his arm had been his sister. Next time, it could be his wife. A pain like a knife thrust tore through her at this thought. Yes, it would be better if they parted before she had to cross that particular bridge.

Too late, she remembered she hadn't asked Traig whether he knew anything about the contents of the letter from Darcy which the doctor was going to give her at the dinner. She debated whether to call him back then decided that she was already too emotionally overwrought to risk it.

If she heard his voice again today she might be tempted to throw caution to the wind and confess that she loved him and wanted to marry him no matter what stood in their way.

As the charts used to warn in the days when sailors believed it was possible to fall off the edge of the world—'there be dragons'. In her case, it was the demon of distrust which lurked at the edge of her world.

She knew how easily he twisted the truth when it suited him. How long would it be before he did it again? He had shown repeatedly that he was unable to keep his promises. And what were marriage vows, after all, but promises?

'What would you do, Dad?' she asked of her father's picture which still held pride of place on her desk. He would probably have told her to go after what she wanted and never mind the consequences, much as Maggie had suggested.

Except that this time, the consequence was likely to be a lifetime of misery, wondering how far she could trust her silver-tongued husband.

Her own self-administered advice still seemed safest—put as much distance between herself and Traig as she could, and soon.

For Darcy's thoughts on the subject, she would have to wait until the dinner to find out what surprises his letter contained.

CHAPTER TEN

THE memorial dinner for Darcy Monroe was the talk of the industry for days beforehand. It seemed as if everyone in the industry was going to be there. Drew's feelings swung wildly between being glad she had agreed to go and wishing that she could avoid it.

Her reluctance had nothing to do with the dinner being in honour of a Monroe. She had come to terms with that virtually since meeting Traig. It was more the prospect of facing Traig in a social setting that bothered her. Somehow, seeing him at the Pacific Centre site or at the office was different. At the dinner, he would be off-duty, laughing, talking . . . dancing with other women. She wasn't sure she wanted to sit and watch him take another woman in his arms.

Her father had always taught her that the best defence was a good offence. She decided it was time for her to start planning her defence.

She began by ordering the first designer gown she had ever bought in her life. Choosing fabrics and attending fittings had always seemed such a waste of time when the stores were crowded with adequate dresses. But she wanted this gown to be more than adequate, so she consulted Maggie who gave her the name of a reliable designer—although not without raising an eyebrow in surprise. Fashion had never concerned Drew overmuch before.

Maggie's eyebrows would have climbed even higher if she could have seen the gown taking shape, but even she was not permitted to glimpse it before the big night.

'You'll see it after the dinner,' Drew repeated when Maggie tried yet again to pry the details out of her.

'Anyone would think it was your debut instead of a dinner for your father's worst enemy,' Maggie sniffed, but Drew could see that she was pleased about Drew's new interest in fashion.

She wouldn't have been so pleased if she had known that Drew's main motive was defiance. In a way, it *was* a kind of debut for her—the unveiling of the new, independent Drew who intended to show Traig that she didn't need him one bit. Only she would know that it was a brave but entirely false façade.

The gown was finished only hours before the dinner. This time Drew had hired one of the designer's assistants to help her dress. She wasn't taking any chances with hot irons on *this* occasion. After all, that was how the fiasco of hiring Traig as her 'wife' got started in the first place.

'You can look now,' the dresser informed her. She had been fidgeting with impatience for over an hour, but neither the dresser nor the hair stylist would let her near a mirror until they were finished.

Now they stood back to give her an uninterrupted view of their handiwork.

'I can't believe it's me,' she said in amazement.

'The dress and the hairstyle only complement your natural advantages,' the dresser assured her.

The woman might be flattering her, but there was no denying the results. The mirror reflected a tall, slender creature who looked more like a Regency shepherdess than a modern-day businesswoman. The gown had been designed to create that effect and had an embroidered satin skirt gathered from the hem into a black satin bow at the waist. Full puff sleeves emphasised the thinness of her arms and a snug velveteen bodice shaped her small waist and plunged provocatively between her well-formed breasts.

The worry of the last few months was reflected in her super-thin figure. This plus her above-average height made her look almost ethereal. The hair stylist had shampooed her hair with a highlighter to bring out its natural sheen, then fluffed it out into a halo around her head. Now she looked years younger and disturbingly vulnerable.

'Madame is pleased?' the hair stylist asked nervously as she surveyed her image in silence.

'Yes, yes of course, I'm delighted,' she assured him and he relaxed visibly, then began to gather up his tools of trade.

She thanked the hair stylist and the dresser, and tipped them generously. When they took their leave, they assured her she would be the belle of the ball tonight.

Kurt Wilder echoed their comments when he arrived to escort her to the dinner. 'All week I've been wishing I was twenty years younger so I could do this evening justice,' he told her. 'Your father would be so proud if he could see you tonight.'

'Do you think so?' she asked in surprise. 'He never took much interest in how I looked, only in how I thought.'

'He might not have said much but he was thrilled all the same,' Kurt said.

This news brought a lump to Drew's throat. So her father had been proud of her after all, enough to mention his pleasure to Kurt. 'I always thought he wished I was a boy,' she said huskily.

'Maybe at first, but not later when you grew into such a lovely young woman. And I do mean lovely.' His appreciative gaze swept her from head to foot.

'At least Inky won't be able to accuse me of not looking feminine tonight,' she smiled.

'I don't think he will be there.'

'What would be more important to him than reporting tonight's doings in his column?'

Kurt grinned. 'His honeymoon.'

Drew's mouth dropped open. 'His what?'

'I take it you haven't heard. Inky ran off with Dolores Hartman. Last I heard they were planning to write a book together.'

'Given the amount of dirt those two have dug over the years, it should be explosive,' she said. Two less likely candidates for marriage than those two she couldn't imagine. They had been sparring through their respective columns for years. It seemed that dividing line between love and hate had been crossed again, Drew thought wryly. Even she and Traig had breached it once or twice but they always pulled back to their own sides. But at least one couple was going to make it work. Silently, she wished the two writers well. 'We'd better be going,' she told Kurt.

The party was already in full swing by the time they reached the harbourside hotel. Drew greeted several people she knew and Kurt introduced her to many others gathered in the crowded lobby.

The envious stares which followed Drew's progress told her she had been wise to dress up for the occasion. She even took a devilish delight in the open-mouthed stares of the society belles. They had come prepared for competition, but not from her it seemed. Several times, they were asked to pose for photographs for the society pages of the newspapers but Drew found that she missed the caustic comments she knew Inky would have made. As Kurt had predicted, neither he nor Dolores put in an appearance.

While they posed for yet another photograph, Kurt said out of the corner of his mouth, 'I'm glad your father can't see this.'

'Why not?'

The photographer released them and they moved on as Kurt said, 'The idea of posing for pictures at a dinner to honour Darcy Monroe! In your Dad's day we weren't even allowed to mention that name in his hearing.'

'I know. But it seems foolish now that they're both gone, doesn't it?'

'That was one reason why I decided to come, for the chance to bury the hatchet. I never agreed with that darned feud as it was. I found out later that Darcy Monroe thought your Dad had pulled out of the deal at the same time he did—each thought the other was to blame and they refused to even talk about it. If Darcy and Andrew had teamed up instead of wrangling, they could have conquered the world.'

If they had teamed up instead of wrangling ... the words seemed significant to Drew, as if Kurt was referring to herself and Traig. But it would never happen now so what was the point of dwelling on it?

She forced a smile to her lips but it never quite reached her eyes as she and Kurt escaped from the lobby at last and made their way to their table.

They had been placed at the front of the room, alongside the head table where Traig, as guest of honour, would sit.

Anxiously, she scanned the room but there was no sign of his tall, commanding figure. She was sure she would have been aware of his presence even without seeing him, so attuned had she become to him lately. But she had no sense of his nearness and took her place at the table with an odd feeling of loss. She hadn't wanted to see him, and yet she had. It was absurd.

Then her senses leapt and she knew he was in the room even before she turned around and saw him.

The occasion was black tie and it suited him to perfection. He looked trimmer and more desirable than ever in his impeccably tailored dinner suit with its gleaming satin lapels. When he raised his head, their eyes met and her breath caught in her throat. But instead of coming over to her he merely inclined his head in acknowledgment and went on talking with the group around him.

At once she felt tears pricking at the backs of her eyes, as if he had rejected her in some way. What a fool she had been to come here, thinking she could be objective about him. It was too soon. Only Kurt's presence at her side and the knowledge that he was enjoying himself, kept her in her seat.

The meal was Chinese which was normally her favourite style of food. But tonight, even delicacies like crisp fried garfish and chicken with snow peas couldn't tempt her jaded palate.

She picked at the dishes with her chopsticks, grateful when the waiter took the plates away. She managed to reply to the questions directed at her by her table companions, but afterwards she couldn't have repeated what answers she gave.

At last the head of the building industry group, which had arranged the dinner, rose to his feet. Gradually, the hum of talk died away as all heads turned towards the top table.

The speaker thanked them all for attending and said a few kind words about Darcy Monroe but declined further comment because, he said, that was the province of the guest of honour—Mr Traig Monroe.

There was enthusiastic applause but Drew didn't join in. Instead, she sat quivering with suppressed emotion, feeling like a wild animal trapped in a hunter's gunsight.

Traig was looking directly towards her, noting that

she made no move to applaud. No doubt he would draw his own conclusions but they would be wrong. It wasn't dislike of him which stilled her hands. It was that applause seemed so inadequate to express the way she felt about him.

When the welcome subsided, Traig leaned towards the microphone. His eulogy for his father must have been rehearsed but he managed to make it sound spontaneous and warm, moving everyone who heard it. Even Drew felt tears on her cheeks when he spoke about the loss they all shared.

'I want to thank the industry group for arranging this dinner in my father's honour,' he concluded. 'They tell me they plan to set up a Darcy Monroe scholarship to encourage youngsters to follow in his footsteps and I'm deeply honoured on behalf of my family. It has made me more aware than ever that we have not only lost a father, but our industry has lost a leader. Thank you.'

This time she did join in the thunderous applause which followed as Traig returned to his seat, but he avoided looking at her.

There were more speeches from people who had known Darcy, then the chairman introduced Alderman Bernard Pierce whom Drew had met when he was a judge of the Walter Burley Griffin Award.

'As you know,' the alderman began, 'I am chairman of the committee which is overseeing the Bicentenary Building programme. One of our projects, Pacific Centre, is already well underway and I would like to commend Miss Drew Dominick on the fine job she's doing with it.'

She flinched as a spotlight sought her out but forced herself to smile in appreciation of the applause which this comment generated. Then the light swung back to Alderman Pierce and Drew sat forward eagerly. He must be going to announce the next project which Dominick's were almost certain to undertake.

'Naturally, you're all anxious to know who will be involved in stage two of the celebration buildings,' he said, deliberately drawing out the tension, 'since tonight's dinner is in memory of Darcy Monroe, I'm even more pleased to announce that the project will be developed by Monroe Investments, headed by Traig Monroe.'

Drew felt stunned. She had been sure that Dominick's would get that contract. They had submitted the most cost-effective tender possible, she was certain. And to have it snatched away by Traig of all people! He must have learned the details of their tender while he was working for her. How else could he have managed to undercut them?

A flush of annoyance spread from her neck up to her hairline. Was there no end to his treachery? She was so angry and preoccupied she hardly heard the rest of the speeches so she was mildly surprised to look up and find that the orchestra was playing and couples were moving towards the dance floor.

'May I have the pleasure of this dance?' a voice asked at her side and she froze as she recognised it.

'No thank you,' she said icily. 'I'm not in the mood for dancing.'

'You won't mind if I borrow your partner, will you Kurt?' Traig asked as if she hadn't spoken.

Kurt chuckled knowingly. 'Go right ahead young Monroe. You're a better match for her energy than I am.'

She cast an appealing look at Kurt but he had already resumed his conversation with the elderly woman on the other side of him. Traig put a hand under her elbow and urged her to her feet. There was no way she could escape without causing a scene, which would embarass Kurt, so she moved unwillingly towards the dance floor.

'Still playing hard to get?' he murmured softly into her ear as he moulded his body against hers.

She tried to move away but was held tightly against him. 'This isn't a game,' she said stiffly.

'Oh yes it is,' he contradicted. 'The trouble is, we've been playing by your rules since it started. I've decided it's time we played by my rules for a while.'

She stiffened in his arms. 'What do you mean?'

He smiled. 'You'll find out.'

He proceeded to make love to her with his body, right there on the dance floor. They were both fully clothed but that was the only thing which saved them from scandalising the other dancers. To an outsider, they were merely moving in time to the music, albeit very very close together. But to Drew it was a total invasion against which she had little defence, as he used every seductive movement he could to force a response from her. To her chagrin, she found herself giving him that response. Her skin flushed and she could hear the blood singing along her veins as her whole body came to vibrant life.

Try as she might to remain aloof, her body betrayed her by shaping itself to his in defiance of her conscious wishes. 'That's the idea,' he murmured encouragingly.

'Why won't you let me go,' she asked despairingly.

'Because we belong together. Like this.'

'No, not like this,' she protested feebly, knowing that her every movement made a liar of her. Her arms had long ago ceased to push against him and had, instead, wound tightly around him. Her breasts felt full and heavy, the nipples tantalised to hard points by the contact. 'This isn't fair.'

'I thought all was fair in love and war.'

Which was this? she asked herself wildly. At last,

disgust at her own weakness gave her the strength to prise herself free. Luckily, the music also ended just then so she had an excuse to move back to her table.

'No you don't, Cinderella,' he said firmly, catching her arm in what looked like a friendly gesture, but was a grip of iron. Irresistibly, he turned her to face him. 'Why won't you give, even a little? You keep forcing me to take what I want.'

Her breathing quickened. In desperation, she said, 'like you took the Bicentenary Project from me?'

He frowned and his hold tightened. 'What's that supposed to mean?'

'It means Dominick's had that contract sewn up. You knew how much I wanted it but you took it. Nobody forces you to do anything—you always take what you want.'

His expression relaxed a little. 'You think I took it from you? Well I didn't. I told you I had a good second-in-command at Monroe's. He prepared our tender. But I thought you wouldn't mind. I had. . . .'

'Don't tell me,' she interrupted sourly. 'You had a good reason for thinking that.'

'As a matter of fact, I had,' he said in a tone of exasperation. 'You see, I knew you'd be too busy to handle that project.'

'Oh? Too busy doing what?'

'Being my wife.'

Astonishment kept her rooted to the spot even though he had released her arm. 'Is this what you mean by playing by your rules? You think that just because you've made up your mind, I have to go along?'

'I was hoping you would want to.'

Was this another of his good reasons? By marrying her he would certainly solve a lot of problems for himself, as well as removing her as competition.

'You've thought it all out, haven't you?' she said bitterly. 'Well, Dad always warned me to beware of takeovers, but I didn't expect one as personal as this.'

As soon as their eyes met and she read the cold anger in his face, she knew she had gone too far. Maybe he had justified the proposal to himself in more reasonable terms. But she had been taught to call a spade a spade.

And a takeover, a takeover.

Unable to face him a moment longer, she hurried to her table and picked up her wrap and bag. When Kurt asked what was wrong, she told him she wasn't feeling well. At once he offered to take her home.

'I'm sorry to spoil your evening,' she said as they waited in the lobby for her car to be brought around.

'Nonsense. I'm too old for all-night revelry anyway,' he assured her. 'I'm more concerned about you.'

'I'll be all right in a minute. I'm feeling better for being out of that crowded room already.'

He looked at her anxiously. 'I hope so. Maybe you should have your doctor call after you get home.'

'I will if I still feel off-colour,' she promised. She glanced around nervously, half expecting Traig to follow them. But there was no sign of him and the doorman assured her their car wouldn't be much longer.

Nevertheless, her nerves were so taut that she jumped when a man put a hand on her arm. 'Miss Dominick?'

She stared at him. 'I'm sorry, have we met?'

'I don't think so, unless it was at the hospital.'

It came back to her now—the letter. She had almost forgotten about it. 'You must be Darcy's doctor,' she said, relieved.

'That's right. I should have contacted you long

before this, when Mr Monroe first gave me the letter
for you. But another doctor took ill and I had to work
double shifts for a while so I completely forgot. Then
I couldn't find the letter and ... well, I hope no
harm's been done by the delay.' He handed her a
sealed envelope.

It was an effort to keep her tone conversational. All
she wanted to do was get as far away from here as
possible, before Traig came after her. 'I'm sure no
harm's been done,' she told the doctor. 'He and my
father had a lifelong misunderstanding so he probably
just wanted to straighten things out.'

The doctor smiled, his relief all too plain. 'I do hope
so. It was nice meeting you, Miss Dominick.'

'Your car is here,' Kurt intervened. Thrusting the
letter into her bag she excused herself from the doctor
and sought the sanctuary of her car where she sank back
against the cushions and closed her eyes. Traig had
actually asked her to marry him. She had no doubt that
she had been right to refuse—his motives were all too
clear. If only it didn't hurt so much to think about.

When they reached her house, Kurt walked her to
her door and again obtained her assurance that she
would call the doctor if she continued to feel ill. Only
after she had promised did he agree to let her driver
take him home.

When they had gone, she wandered around the
living room in a daze, letting her wrap lie where it fell
and tossing her handbag on to the nearest chair. Traig
had asked her to marry him. The fact went round and
round in her head until she felt dizzy.

Thank goodness she had found the strength to
refuse. After the way he'd aroused her on the dance
floor, she had very nearly said yes—which was
probably his idea all along. The memory of his body
aligned with hers as they danced sent a shiver down

her spine. Even now, she could feel the lean hardness of him pressed intimately against her.

How easy it would have been to say yes—except that he wanted a takeover, which she couldn't agree to. She had been brought up believing that marriage should be an equal partnership, but that wasn't what Traig had in mind, she was sure.

She poured herself a brandy and curled up on the couch, absently stroking Bosun who jumped up beside her. Belatedly, she remembered the letter the doctor had given her. For a moment, she was tempted to burn it unopened. She didn't need any more interference in her life by a Monroe.

Finally, curiosity got the better of her. She took the letter out of her bag and ran a fingernail along the envelope, slitting it.

Her hands trembled as she unfolded the sheets of paper which bore the hospital letterhead. Darcy's writing showed how ill he had been when he wrote it. The spidery writing sprawled all over the page as if he had had difficulty controlling the pen.

At first she could hardly decipher the message but gradually she became accustomed to the writing.

'*My dear Drew* (it said),
I had hoped to tell you this myself but I fear I may not live long enough or retain command of my faculties. Already I am frustrated because I cannot say all that is in my mind.'

She had been right, she thought, he had been a prisoner inside his body during those last weeks. How terrible it must have been for him. Her eyes misted and she had to pause for a moment, before reading on.

'*After he joined your firm* (Darcy continued), *Garth Dangerfield told me he had been wrongly treated by my son who, he said, was in league with you. Since Traig has never shown an interest in my business, this was not hard to believe.*

  'Forgive an old man, Drew, but I agreed to help Garth to make mischief for you. I gave him the name of an importer who supplied inferior materials and helped Garth to place an order in your name, knowing it would make trouble for you.

  'Then I fell ill and Traig spent days sitting and talking to me, although he didn't know I could hear. I realised how much you meant to him and I knew what a terrible thing I had done.

  'I knew then that you were not your father, and that if you and Traig had a chance of happiness together, I was wrong to interfere.

  'Believe me, I tried to tell you and set things right but my mind is not what it was. So I am writing this while I still can. Later may be too late.

  'I only hope it won't be too late for you and Traig. My blessings to you both.'

It was signed, Darcy Monroe.

'Oh, Bosun,' she breathed, her tears splashing on to the bewildered dog's coat. 'How could I have been such an idiot?'

Darcy had been the 'Mr Monroe' of the letters Garth had shown her—not Traig at all. It was 'Garth . . . steel' Darcy had been saying to her at the last, not 'steal' as she'd thought. He had been trying to tell her that he and Garth were behind the steel shipment.

If only she had received the letter sooner! Now it was too late, as Darcy had feared. She had turned down Traig's proposal and the anger and hurt in his eyes were burned on her memory. She had accused him of terrible things, refusing to believe his explanations.

Even if she went to him now and told him she knew the whole story, he would still despise her as he had every right to do. She had known all along that lack of trust was the main obstacle to their happiness. What she hadn't been able to see was that the lack of trust was all on her side. His word that he had done her no harm had not been good enough for her. He would think it despicable that she only trusted him when she had proof.

All the tears she had refused to shed came raining down now, more for Traig and the way she had treated him, than for herself and all she had lost. To Bosun, she murmured in despair, 'Oh ye of little faith—that's me, pal.'

The world around her was turquoise, jade and aquamarine, but even the beauty of Honeymoon Island wasn't enough to dull the pain of the last weeks.

Coming here had seemed like a good idea when Maggie suggested it a couple of days after the memorial dinner. She had been concerned about Drew's pallor and lack of interest in everything, fearing that she was becoming ill again.

Drew had protested that she was fine but Maggie had kept on until she finally agreed to come to the island to regain her health.

Now, she wasn't sure it had been wise. At every turn the island dredged up memories of the time she had spent here with Traig. One day, she went walking and came upon the depression in the sand which their bodies had hollowed out as a nest for their shared passion. A pain like a knife thrust went through her at the sight.

Returning to the beach house she found a t-shirt he had left behind. Childishly, she took it to bed with her and soaked it with her tears. In the morning, she awoke still cradling it.

Although she told herself it was foolish and useless, she still felt compelled to wear the t-shirt over her bikini when she set off on her morning walk.

The cicadas singing in the underbrush did their best to lull her, and the reef fish leaping in the crystal waters of the lagoon put on a special show for her, but nothing seemed to assuage the pain inside her.

At every turn she was reminded of being here with Traig. Even the waves seemed to whisper his name.

It was all so useless. She had lost him and she may as well accept it and go on living. The idea of coming to the island was to forget the problems she had left behind, she reminded herself. She would have to stop dwelling on them. Taking a stick, she began to draw in the sand as she had done when she was small. But when she finished, the letters had somehow turned into his name.

To dispel her gloom she set off to run around the island, throwing her arms out to her sides like an athlete. The wind ruffled her hair and the movement felt cathartic, but she knew that sooner or later she would have to stop running.

She came up short as she reached a stretch of deserted beach. On the sand was a row of unmistakably human footprints. Who's could they be? The caretaker, Oliver Daintree, had gone away on business soon after she arrived. Then she glimpsed a cruiser anchored off a headland nearby. Damn! The last thing she wanted now was visitors. Even the task of ordering them off her island seemed too much.

But the figure which strode towards her was no tourist. She would have known that tall, commanding figure anywhere.

'Hello, Drew,' he said quietly.

She found her voice with an effort. 'Hello, Traig. What are you doing here?'

'Looking for you.'

'Now I know how Robinson Crusoe felt when he found Man Friday on his island,' she said with an attempt at lightness. She didn't want to ask him what his last remark meant in case it wasn't an answer she could bear.

'I suppose there are similarities,' he agreed. 'Man Friday was a slave after all.'

She could hardly breathe for the tight band which had clamped itself around her chest. 'What are you a slave to?'

'To you. To love,' he responded.

The eyes she turned to him were large with a hopefulness she had thought was gone for ever. 'Please don't tease me,' she begged.

'I'm not. I mean every word,' he vowed. 'Oh, Drew, I had to come. I couldn't let another day go by without seeing you.'

'Even after all the terrible things I accused you of?'

'Even then. You can say whatever you like to me, as long as you don't say I have to leave.'

She sank down on to a rock, her spray-dampened t-shirt outlining every curve of her body. 'But I don't want you to leave,' she whispered.

In an instant, he was on his knees beside her, oblivious of the waves lapping at his trouser legs. 'What did you say?'

'I said I don't want you to leave—ever.'

His eyes shone. 'You really mean that?'

She nodded. 'Yes, but I don't think you'll want to stay when I tell you what a fool I've been. Darcy wrote me a letter but I received it too late. He explained that he and Garth were the ones who sabotaged the steel shipment, not you. Oh, Traig, I'm so sorry. I didn't recognise the truth until I had my nose rubbed in it.'

'But you know it now. That's what matters,' he said gently.

She turned luminous eyes on him. 'Then you'll forgive me for not trusting you?'

'It wasn't all on your side,' he reminded her. 'I believed you were in league with Garth until I got to know you. Now I do, I can forgive you anything as long as you'll say you love me and will marry me.'

'Oh, Traig, I do love you and I will marry you. I was a fool to turn you down the first time.'

There was a burning hunger in his kiss which fired her own responses until she was trembling with desire. But drugged as she was with passion, she made herself pull away from him. 'There is something more.'

'What's that?' he asked, frustration in his tone.

'Our marriage has to be a merger, not a takeover,' she said firmly.

His eyes sparkled with amusement but he said seriously, 'That was one mistake I made. If I made my first offer sound like a takeover, I'm sorry. I want ours to be an equal partnership in every sense—partner.'

Something in his tone told her he meant it. From now on their's would be a partnership. It would take time before they learned to trust one another completely, but they had already learned their first painful lesson.

'Is that the only item on the agenda?' he asked in the same caressing tone.

'No. There's one more thing—we have to decide who is going to be "wife".'

He grinned, warming her in the glow of his smile. 'I think I've had that job long enough, don't you?'

'Man and wife, that's you,' she teased.

'Not me any more, it applies to both of us from here on,' he amended. 'Anything else?'

Suddenly shy, she shook her head.

'Then I move that we adjourn this meeting while I take stock of my new partner,' he said, his voice husky with desire.

She smiled langorously, 'I'll second that.'

It was a meeting which would have raised eyebrows had it taken place in a boardroom, but here on the beach, when they slid down on to the warm sand and he covered her pliant body with his, the golden orb of the sun was the only witness to the merger.

There were no dissenting votes.